EMPOWERED

THE ORACLE CHRONICLES
BOOK 3

BY

MONI BOYCE

LOVE
SNACKS
PUBLISHING

Love Snacks Publishing, LLC

Empowered: The Oracle Chronicles © 2019 Shaquana M. Boyce

www.lovesnackspublishing.com

First Edition
ISBN: 978-1-7333937-3-7

Book cover design by: Mallory Rock of Rock Solid Book Design

EMPOWERED

CHAPTER 1

Willow

"**ANCESTORS, WE ASK** that you will welcome Mathilda with open arms and watch over her." Alistair's voice shook and tears fell from his bloodshot eyes.

Mathilda's burial was a somber affair. Everyone's emotions were still raw, open wounds and jagged edges. When Alistair, Mathilda's father, invoked the ancestors to watch over her, Zoriana sobbed loudly. Anxious seconds had ticked by with Willow afraid that Zoriana would hurl herself on her daughter's casket and demand to be buried alive with her. A few times, glimpses of Zoriana's white hot anger poked through the heavy cloak of her consuming grief, and Willow nearly felt sorry for Morgana. Whatever hell Zoriana had planned for her would be unimaginable.

Again, Willow thought how cruel it was that a parent should have to bury a child. It had been hard at nine years-old to watch her mother be lowered six feet into the earth, but she couldn't imagine the heartache, agony and rage that could be borne of having to bury a part of yourself, a child that had grown in your womb and gathered life and sustenance from your body for nine months. A shiver ran up her spine at the thought and she wrapped her arms around her body. Eli draped his arm across her shoulders, and she leaned into him.

After the ceremony he teleported them to the Walker house. As they walked to his rooms, she saw the hint of a purplish discoloration that marked his neck peeking out above his collar. Earlier, when he dressed for the funeral after the daily sparring match with Phaedra, she'd seen the fresh bruises he sported. If he wanted to he could choose to heal them or make them disappear, but she knew he wore the blue-black bruises as penance for not being there to save Mathilda.

They entered his apartment in silence. He was already tugging off his tie as he walked towards the bedroom. She lingered in the living room. The fact that she had yet to share with everyone her disturbing conversation with Morgana before everything happened weighed on her. Making the decision that she could no longer wait, she entered the bedroom.

Eli looked up at her as his nimble fingers unbuttoned his shirt.

"We need to talk."

He looked at her with his eyes full of questions.

"What I mean is that I need to talk to all of you. There are things that Morgana told me in the tomb that I haven't shared."

He opened up his mouth to say something, and she hurried along in her explanation.

"Before you ask, I haven't said anything before now because it didn't seem like the right time... everyone was grieving... everyone is still grieving, but I can't wait any longer." Her fingers twisted themselves in knots as she looked at him.

His mouth was set in a grim line as he continued to change his clothes, moving from his funeral attire to jeans and a t-shirt. "I'll gather everyone." He slipped his shirt over his head. "The sooner we know everything, the quicker we can act."

A rush of relief flooded her. She hadn't realized how tired she was of carrying all of that around. Maybe she'd been tired of carrying everything around alone?

"You know where to find us?" He kissed her forehead and left the room.

All she could do was nod as anxiety assailed her over how the others would handle the information.

After Eli left to round up the others, she stripped off her dress and put on jeans and a tank top. Unconsciously, her fingers found their way to the snake pendant that dangled from her necklace. She rubbed the silver piece of jewelry and briefly thought of her mother. The day after Mathilda was killed she'd finished reading all of her mother's letters, wanting to see if there was anything contained in the letters that might have been useful in preventing her or Ulrik's death. It was a relief and a burden not to have found anything within the letters. Twenty minutes later, she walked into the room that had come to be known as their training room. Phaedra and Eli stood, and Max sat in a chair. It felt weird to walk into the room and not see the whole group. She shut the door behind her, not bothering to offer a smile like she normally would have. They'd grown quiet the minute she entered the room. It felt like an endless journey as she crossed the room and approached them, their eyes watching her every step.

"Elias said you wanted to share some things about Morgana." Phaedra jumped right into it.

She couldn't blame her, but she took a moment to check on Max. "How are you feeling?"

He gave her one of his signature Max smiles. "I'm good. All the silver is finally out of my system." The good news about his health uplifted her spirit.

Her attention went back to Phaedra. "Yes, I do... Morgana said some things before..." She trailed off. The silence in the room was heavy with her unsaid words. She cleared her throat and continued on. "Morgana said some troubling things... some things were regarding Mathilda."

"What did that venomous bitch have to say about Mathilda?"

Everyone's heads whipped around to find Zoriana standing in the doorway. Her eyes were red-rimmed and puffy, but she looked like a warrior, ready to fight.

"Zoriana... we hadn't expected you to..." Eli started, before she cut him off.

"To what?" She looked at each of them. "I'm still part of The Protectors right? A meeting was called, and I'm here. I want to hear what that piece of trash had to say about my daughter." Her chest rose and fell in agitation, and the fierce, rigid stance she erected belied the well of grief Willow knew was right below the surface. The only thing that gave her away, were the tears that glistened in her eyes. "Go on Willow, what were you saying?"

There was a long pause before Willow shook herself from her stupor and continued on. "Morgana mentioned how after Mathilda's big blow up with you... that we all overheard..." Willow's eyes darted over to Zoriana for a brief second to gauge her reaction. When she saw the hard scowl she wore she dropped her gaze and kept talking. "When Mathilda fled into the woods that day, she stumbled on Morgana talking to Killian. She couldn't let her get back to camp and tell us what she saw so she used a spell to put

Mathilda to sleep." She'd resumed looking at each of them during different parts of her story, with the exception of Zoriana. The others grew upset over what she revealed.

"How was she able to speak to Killian without him figuring out where we were or using another witch to figure it out?" Phaedra asked the practical question.

"She said she'd devised a way. I assumed it was some sort of spell. I didn't ask her to elaborate." It was hard keeping the irritation at the question out of her tone. Her frustration wasn't with Phaedra. It was more so directed at herself. Morgana had been forthcoming with so many answers that night. Why hadn't she thought to ask that question? When she was sure no one else was about to lob another question at her, she picked up where she left off. "She said she gave Mathilda a forget potion."

The minute she said that Eli, Phaedra and Zoriana verbally and mentally began to chastise themselves.

"How did I not see it?" Zoriana said out loud, but to no one in particular. She looked off and appeared to be thinking about the different moments when she should have caught onto something being wrong.

"Don't beat yourself up. She had us all fooled." Willow tried to offer. It was easier to say than to do. They'd all been playing this 'what if' game since everything had happened. *What if I'd realized sooner? What if I'd just come into the tomb earlier? What if I'd seen Morgana for who she really is?*

She more than anyone had been feeling that there was more she could have done. She'd been right there in the cave when it happened.

"Dosing her with the forget potion allowed her to keep Mathilda from remembering."

"The forget potion explains a piece of that, but not why Mathilda stayed angry so long." Phaedra theorized once again.

"Morgana brewed another potion that would keep her angry at you." This time she looked directly at Zoriana when she spoke. "She knew if she kept the feud going and Mathilda stayed upset with you..."

A tear fell down Zoriana's cheek before she finished Willow's sentence, "... she'd never forgive me or want to confide in me."

"Plus, it would allow her to stay close and keep tabs, in case any of the potions ever seemed like they were wearing off." It was agonizing watching Zoriana have the revelation that her daughter was kept from reconciling with her by a person she'd trusted and loved.

"She said Ulrik recognized the effects of the potion the day at the apartment in Egypt. It was one of the reason's she killed him. Besides the fact that Killian wanted him dead for a while."

Another wave of sadness engulfed them as they thought about their fallen friend. Even though they'd known him only for a short while, he'd proven to be a true ally, despite being a vampire. Willow thought of her goodbye to Anippe before they finally left Egypt. The young woman was bereft over his loss.

"There's more. She originally tried to kill Ulrik the day we fought Katana and her pack of vampires at the ruins."

"That explains the weird look on his face when he covered for her. He was probably trying to figure out if it was in his head, a mistake or if she'd really tried to kill him." Eli mused over the situation. "I wished he'd shared his suspicion with us."

Zoriana snorted. "He probably didn't think he could since she was one of us." At saying the words 'one of us', Zoriana looked like she wanted to spit, like the words had a left a bad taste in her mouth. "How do you think we would have reacted to his accusation? He knew we already considered him an outsider. Sharing his conspiracy theory with us at that point would have ostracized him even further. The assumption about one of our own..." She shook her head. "He was trying to gather more clues, more evidence before he would approach with something that damning so we wouldn't turn on him."

No one could deny that Zoriana was right. If Ulrik had come to them with that tale they would have taken up weapons against him to defend Morgana.

Max seemed to land on something that was puzzling him. "Her wanting to kill Ulrik at that time makes sense, but why hurt the other vampires during that fight if she was working with them?"

"That's where it gets interesting. Killian must have been growing impatient with Morgana, because he'd sent Katana there to grab the book and me. If she'd been successful, whatever deal they'd struck would have been dead in the water. Morgana hurt them that day to force Katana to leave. She said that if she provided Killian with The Book of Prophecy and me, then he would reward her with what she wanted. When I asked what that was and why she would betray all of us, she just old me we would find out soon enough."

Everything she shared so far only seemed to raise more questions for everyone. She'd hoped that someone might have some insight, but it was clear, whatever answers they were going to find were outside the group. There was just one last thought she needed to share.

"One of the things that confused me about that conversation was the way she reacted to your relationship, your bond with Mathilda. It was like she was envious of the closeness you guys shared as mother and daughter." She addressed Zoriana before turning to Eli. "I know you said she was an orphan, but maybe there is something in Morgana's past or something about her parents that might help shed light on why she did this."

"I know exactly who's going to give us answers." The determined look on Eli's face let her know that they would get the answers they sought.

CHAPTER 2

Eli

THERE WOULDN'T BE any following protocol today. They deserved answers and wanted them now. The moment he'd heard Willow mention Morgana being jealous of the bond between Zoriana and Mathilda, he knew The Council would have more information. Maybe not all of them, but he was certain his father and Cora would know about her parentage or if there was anything there worth taking a look at. They weren't leaving that chamber until the Elders spilled their guts. If there was stuff they knew that they'd kept hidden, they were just as responsible for Mathilda's death as Morgana.

Forcefully, he pushed open the door and walked into the room with the others right behind him. Archie severely out of breath staggered into the room a few seconds later.

"I tried..." He wheezed out. "I tried to stop..." The old man bent over and gulped in air. Everyone in the room waited patiently for him to catch his breath. "I tried to stop them since they didn't have an appointment."

His father had stood from his chair the minute they marched in unannounced. "It's fine Archibald. We'll take it from here."

Archie's face was still flushed and red as he gave Eli a withering look before he departed. Any other day Eli would have smirked or laughed, but not today.

"What's the meaning of this intrusion?" His father's tone started out a bit hostile, but when his eyes landed on Zoriana the harshness evaporated.

Cora sat upon the dais next to his father. She didn't seem the least bit surprised by their unanticipated arrival. Maybe for her it wasn't unexpected.

Before he could launch into the reason behind their abrupt arrival, his father spoke. "We wish to offer you our condolences..." He must have heard how canned and rehearsed he sounded, like a politician and not like a grieving uncle because he cleared his throat and his voice sounded sincere before he spoke again. "I can't tell you how saddened Josephine and I are over the loss of Mathilda. She was such a vibrant young woman... I know she would have gone on to do wonderful things."

Zoriana stood next to him. Her body vibrated with a mixture of grief and anger that ran through her veins. He wasn't looking at her, but was sure she was doing her best to display a measure of calm and control she didn't quite feel. It was evident when she found them discussing Morgana. She gave his father a curt nod. He used that time to explain why they were there.

"I believe we're owed some answers." He stared into his father's eyes.

"Answers to what?"

Does he really want to play this game?

The smartass remark died on his lips when Cora opened her mouth.

"They're here for answers about Morgana." In her eyes, he saw that she knew this day would come. What secrets had the old crone kept?

At her words, his father slowly sat down in his seat. It seemed Cora wasn't the only one that had been keeping secrets. Suddenly, his father looked ten years older.

"What do you want to know?" Cora asked with the regalness of a queen holding court.

"Everything." Willow had her arms folded across her chest as she made the demand.

He glared at Cora waiting for her to tell them that story was off limits; that they didn't have a right to know. So he was a little surprised when she didn't try and argue.

"Morgana's lineage is descended from Morgan Le Fay."

The shocked gasps that came from Willow and the others mirrored his own dismay.

"You knew she had an ancestor notorious for being an evil sorceress and you didn't think we should know that?" There was no reason to hide the incredulity that surely marked his face. "Why?"

Cora was unfazed by his anger. "I'm afraid there is more about this story that you won't like."

What could possibly be worse than Morgana having Morgan fucking Le Fay as an ancestor? It was like having Hitler or Charles Manson as part of your family tree. None of them said anything as they waited for Cora to drop the bomb and decimate all of them.

"Over twenty years ago, a Walker witch became consumed with learning black magic, even though she knew it was forbidden."

Where is she going with all of this? It was hard not to feel impatient about Cora telling what sounded like a bedtime story.

Her voice was the only sound that could be heard in the room. "She sought outside sources to feed her thirst and hunger. In doing so, she met Killian, king of the vampires who was looking for a witch to conspire with despite the laws he'd set in place for those of his kind not to have dealings with other supernaturals."

They all listened raptly as she wove her tale.

"Killian had come into possession of an ancient Grimoire and was in need of a witch to open the book since a spell had been placed on it to keep it from being opened by anyone other than a witch." Coughs racked Cora's body for countless seconds. His father handed her a glass of water, and she drank it down while they all looked on, anxious for her to continue.

She cleared her throat and picked up the story. "It was exactly what she'd been looking for a book filled with black magic. In exchange for the book, she agreed to work for him. She practiced the spells and became quite the sorceress. Like anyone with a heart consumed with darkness, she began to thirst for power and wanted to raise followers, so she returned to Walker house intent on sowing her seeds and enticing those witches to join her that were also thirsty for power and to learn black magic."

Even though Zoriana was slightly behind him, he could feel her hostility in the very air around him, because they both knew where Cora's story was heading.

"Soon she was pitting friend against friend, and eventually, the rumblings and disquiet boiled over one day, resulting in what we now know as The Black Magic Rebellion, some called it an uprising. No matter the side you chose, many lost their lives during the battle."

Nothing needed to be said. They all knew some people in the room had lost loved ones. One of them was standing near him.

"When it was all over, she along with anyone that had chosen her side were stripped of their ancestral magic and sentenced to death."

Willow spoke up this time. "She could have gone anywhere to gather witches for her cause and avoid bloodshed. Why come back here, a place she knew already condemned black magic?"

"She had to come back for her baby, a daughter."

The minute the words left Cora's mouth, he felt like he'd been gut punched. His head was swimming with the revelation. There was no need to turn and gauge the others' reactions. He knew they were just as shocked as he was. "Morgana's mother was the witch responsible for the Black Magic Rebellion?" He was nearly breathless when he asked the question. No wonder she'd betrayed them all. The coven was responsible for killing her mother.

Before Cora or any other Elder could respond, another voice exploded in the stillness of the room.

"You let that toxic bitch stay here knowing she might grow up and become her mother?" The rage that bled from Zoriana, clogged the air in the room. "Her mother led the rebellion that killed my parents. For all I know, they died by her hand." Her breath became a bit labored as she seemed to suffocate on her own wrath. "You let me eat with that woman's offspring, come to care about her, bleed with her, all for her to turn around and kill my kid... be just what nature told you she would be from the moment she was born... her mother's daughter?"

The others must have heard the wildness in her voice the same as he did because Phaedra edged closer. He'd taken a few steps back until he was standing beside her.

"We believed that just as history provided variations on Morgan Le Fay's dual nature and her potential for both good and evil, that Morgana stood that same chance and would choose good over evil." Cora stated it so matter-of-fact and clinical like they were discussing a test subject and not someone that had just killed a member of their team.

"You believed... you believed?" Zoriana's voice rose, along with her outrage. Her hand twitched at her side. The look in her eyes told him that she was capable of anything at this moment. He feared she was about to do something she would regret.

"Zoriana, listen to me. We're all angry over what we just heard, but let's take a minute." His eyes met Phaedra and knew that one of them would put her to sleep if they had to so she wouldn't do anything stupid.

"You have every right to be angry over the things that were hidden from us..." What could he say to make her stop plotting whatever she'd gotten into her head? "It's not worth it..." His voice grew quiet and full of emotion. "I don't want to see you stripped like I was."

At his words, she seemed to return to herself, her eyes lost the thunderous black look they'd had a moment ago. When she glanced at him, he could see the grief outweighing the fury. Once he was sure Zoriana was under control, he turned back to The Elders. "I think we can all agree that Morgana not only did all of this to somehow get even for her mother's death, but to get the Grimoire that must still be in Killian's possession. Clearly, she wants to follow in her mother's footsteps."

If only the Elders had shared all of this with Morgana and all of them when she'd come of an age to understand and come to terms with it, instead of making it some dirty secret. Maybe history wouldn't be getting ready to repeat itself.

"Not only are we now contending with Killian, but a dangerous witch with a vendetta that more than likely has access to a Grimoire with magic that could be very powerful." Phaedra's voice cut through the white noise in his head. She was right. They now had two enemies that would be working against them.

"And they have The Book of Prophecy." Willow's voice was full of disquiet when she spoke.

After she spoke, he walked over to her. "It's not your fault." He whispered the words for only her ears as he pulled her into his body for comfort. It wasn't a secret that she felt responsible for Mathilda's death and the book being taken. Even though he'd assured her she'd done the only thing she could, she hadn't been able to accept that.

Everything The Elders revealed had him on edge. Yes, they'd used spells to restrict Morgana's access to Walker house, but she knew everything. What was to stop her from trying to come back here to exact her vengeance and bring Killian and his minions with her? Not only that, she more than likely had a plethora of black magic spells and... Walker hereditary magic. His heart ached knowing he did not.

On impulse he shouted out to The Council. "Reinstate me to The Protectors." The statement was issued as an order. He was banking on The Council feeling guilty over the hand they'd played in everything that happened that they would agree. "You know it's the right thing to do... we're down three people as it is. At least if I'm back, then... we're only down two." The words hurt to say. Saying them felt like choking down dry food that you needed a glass of water for afterwards.

"Also..." he inhaled deeply and then released it in a quick breath right before he rushed out his next words. "I want you to give me back my hereditary magic."

Some of The Council members wore shocked and outraged expressions. Rumbling filled the room, but he plowed on with an explanation. "Morgana still has the power of the ancestors..." This statement made some of the irate members clamp their mouths shut. "I can't be reinstated and face her without having the full use of my magic. If we're going to defeat Killian and Morgana, I need my hereditary magic restored."

Who could argue with that? For charged seconds, no one said a word. Willow took his hand in hers as they waited.

"We'll take it into consideration." His father looked at him with weary eyes while he issued the compromise. There was no need to continue the argument if they were willing to take it under advisement. He wouldn't let them wait too long to come to a decision.

CHAPTER 3

Willow

UNTIL ELI HAD voiced aloud the fact that Morgana still had her hereditary magic, Willow hadn't thought about just how powerful an opponent she would be when they finally encountered her again. It wasn't a matter of if they saw her again; it was a matter of when. With the Walker ancestors at her back, Killian at her side, this Grimoire everyone spoke of that contained powerful black magic spells and what was clearly a need to settle the score over the coven killing her mother, Morgana was going to be formidable.

All of the times she'd whined and complained about training, all of the times she'd wanted to throw in the towel because things were too hard fled the moment she thought about what they faced. No longer could she afford to not get this right, not master these skills, abilities and what was ultimately her birthright. Playtime was over. If she was going to survive this or at the very least, avenge Mathilda, it was going to take all the discipline and anger she had.

"Let's train now."

Eli's steps halted as she came to stand in front of him. The others had gone their separate ways after they left The Council Chamber.

"Right this very minute?" His eyes probed her face.

"Yes, right now. You said so yourself that Morgana is going to be dangerous when we see her again. I have to get ready." She let out a breath. "I won't be caught off guard again... I won't let another person die because I wasn't prepared." The last few words came out much quieter.

"Okay."

Several minutes after changing their clothes for workout gear, they were in the training room. Eli tossed her a stave. "We'll start with weapons training." He took a stave off the wall and stood across from her.

Immediately she dropped into a crouch with the stave raised. "I'm ready."

He smiled and for a minute, it felt like life before Mathilda's death. She hadn't seen him smile like that in weeks... she was still planning to kick his butt though. He did a few fancy maneuvers with his stave and then they were attacking each other. With every sound of their wooden sticks ricocheting off each other, she began to realize why he and Phaedra did this often. It really did help relieve some of the pent up anger and sadness that seemed to settle into her bones lately.

In the midst of their sparring, she couldn't help grinning. Her thoughts remembered a time when she would have been knocked to the ground from the first blow of her opponent. Just as she was feeling confident, he used his stave to expertly swipe her feet out from under her. Since her thoughts had wandered off, she didn't have time to react and found herself flat on her back, the breath momentarily knocked out of her. She lay there gazing up at the ceiling. When Eli stood over her and held out his hand to help her up, she took it without anger and let him pull her to her feet.

He looked surprised at her silence and easy acceptance of his help. Usually, she was spitting and hissing like a cat over being bested and then offered help. Today was a new day.

"Thanks." She returned to her crouch. "Let's go again."

For the next couple hours they sparred. Each match grew longer, but every time she was the one that ended up on her back. A couple times after a defeat, she smacked the mat in frustration, but then would mentally chastise and remind herself that she couldn't grow angry because if she went into the next round like that she would surely lose. She would reset her mind and graciously accept Eli's outstretched hand, and they would go again. By the time their session came to a close, she hadn't won a match, but her endurance and stamina were increasing.

Baby steps.

"I'm proud of you." Eli's voice pulled her from her thoughts. "You were great today." His eyes were lit up with adoration.

She wrinkled her nose at him as he pulled her into his side. "I was? But, I didn't win even one match."

His lips grazed her forehead in a sweet kiss. "True, but more importantly, you didn't let your emotions get the better of you."

When he pulled back to look at her again, the look in his eyes made her want to throw him to the ground and sex him right here in this room, and that's exactly what she would have done if Phaedra and Zoriana hadn't entered with Max in tow.

Both of them turned to see who had intruded.

"We need to pay Samson a visit." Phaedra was clearly the ringleader. Zoriana and Max flanked her on either side. None of them seemed apologetic about interrupting them.

"Why do we need to see Samson?" Eli was just as confused as she was about why they wanted to see him again.

This time Zoriana spoke up, "Have you forgotten that Morgana only had weapons that could have come from him?"

Willow's eyes rested on Max for a few seconds when she remembered watching the silver course through his veins in that tomb that could have very well become his final resting place. A low growl came from Max. He had every right to be angry. She didn't know Samson well enough to feel sorry for him, but when she looked at the three people standing before her with fury blazing in their eyes she felt a small ounce of sympathy for the man.

In some past life she knew nothing about, Samson may have been Eli's friend, but it didn't trump his current bond and connection with the people standing in front of him that he'd fought with and spilled blood for. "We'll be ready to go in fifteen minutes."

As promised, in fifteen minutes they both showered and donned fresh clothes. Willow now found herself on Protector's motor home 2.0. Solemnly, she looked around the interior of the RV. Mathilda's presence seemed to fill the space. In her mind, she could see the young girl seated at the table dealing cards and laughing or animatedly talking about some potion she'd perfected. When Max's gaze lingered on the bench seat next to the window, she knew she wasn't the only one affected.

Zoriana grabbed the passenger seat and did not turn her head to look back. She couldn't blame her. This was hard. No matter how many times they might use their magic to change the RV and its exterior or interior,

Mathilda was indelibly stamped all over it. At some point, when the wounds weren't so fresh they might welcome the parts of her that lingered behind, but today wasn't that day.

Max took the driver's seat so that Phaedra and Eli could talk. Once the vehicle rumbled to life and headed out onto the road, she sat silently listening to their conversation.

"We're down two members. We have to figure out..." Phaedra had barely completed the thought before Eli cut her off.

"I think it's too soon to be considering replacing Mathilda..." He glanced towards the front of the motor home to see if Zoriana had heard anything. When he was sure she hadn't, he continued, but dropped his voice. "How do you think Zoriana is going to feel when we bring in someone new so soon?"

It was one of the first times since she'd met them that she saw a flash of anger in Phaedra's eyes that was directed at Eli. In the same moment, the anger disappeared before the woman spoke.

"I hope she'll be thinking like a Protector..." Her words were the world weary, sage words of a general who'd seen one too many battles.

If you didn't know her on a deeper level, it was easy to see how someone could easily be fooled by her no nonsense attitude and expressionless face, but Willow had come to notice that Phaedra wore her emotion in other ways. She sported the same bruises that Eli did, but the depth of her emotion she wore in her eyes. She did her best to hide it, but every now and then a glimmer of her emotions slipped through. What she saw reflected there now made her own eyes well up with tears.

"I miss her too... I grieve for her too, but..." There was that emotion trying to creep in. Phaedra swallowed her feelings, until they were probably dissolved by the acids in her stomach. "We still have a job to do." She took a breath. "It is unfair that life must go on. This threat, this fight isn't going to stop because we had a loss."

"She's right." It took a minute for Willow to realize it was her agreeing with Phaedra. Both of them were gawking at her. "She's right." She stated again with more surety as she sat up straighter. "I wish we had more time to only focus on healing. I know we all need that, but Killian is counting on the fact that we'll be licking our wounds. Now is not the time to grow weak." A month ago, she would have called Phaedra all sorts of colorful names and said she was callous and heartless, but now she knew that the woman was being pragmatic. It might be difficult, but right now it's the way they all needed to be if they were going to survive.

"Okay." Eli looked between the two of them. "We'll start the process to fill the two spaces when we get back."

His eyes wandered once again towards Zoriana. "I'll break the news to Zoriana."

She reached across the table and took his hand in hers. It wasn't going to be easy to break the news to Zoriana. He smiled at the gesture and gave her hand a gentle squeeze of thanks. The rest of the trip they rode in silence. Everyone was deep in their own thoughts.

By the time they pulled up to Samson's warehouse, she was sure their rage, anguish and mourning had festered into a fine simmering stew that had them all ready to become Samson's worst nightmare. They got off the motor home with purpose. The armed men that guarded the warehouse didn't stand a chance. Before one of them could ask them to state their business, Zoriana made quick work of putting them down. Their unconscious bodies dropped to the ground in a deep sleep, the weapons clattering when they struck the pavement.

When they stormed inside, Phaedra took care of the men that guarded the inside. Before Samson could grab for a nearby weapon, Eli pinned his large frame to the wall and held him immobile.

"What... did you... do to my men?" Samson stammered, while he attempted to break free of the magical spell Eli was using against him.

"Don't worry. They're still alive." Zoriana bit out.

When Eli released him, Samson fell to the ground. Before he could get to his feet Phaedra and Max were on him. The punch Max delivered to his gut made Willow wince in pain. If he'd delivered the same punch while he was in his wolf form, she was sure it would have gone right through him, even a man of Samson's stature wouldn't have survived it. Considering the animosity the two held for each other during their last visit, it was no surprise that there was no love lost between them now. Max was about to aim for the kidneys on his next punch, but Phaedra stopped him. Her magic twisted Samson to face her.

"When did Morgana come back here? Why did you sell her weapons we'd refused last time we were here?" The questions came out in rapid succession.

Suddenly, Willow had a strong sense of déjà vu. She shook her head to clear it as she watched Phaedra shout more questions at Samson. No matter what she did, the feeling wouldn't go away... and then it hit her. She had seen this before, in a vision. The first time she could clearly see the visions that she had. It had been one of the first times the visions had slowed down enough for her to process them. Right before Eli rejected her. If only she could have heard Phaedra's words during the vision, maybe she could have stopped Mathilda's death.

Phaedra's harsh yell brought her back to the present.

Samson was still trying to catch his breath after Max's blow. "I don't know... I don't know what you're talking about. I thought she'd been sent back here to acquire more weapons."

"That gun with the silver bullets you sold her nearly killed Max." In her anger, Phaedra used her magic and hurled Samson against the wall.

Samson slowly staggered to his feet, clutching his stomach. "What happened?" He wheezed before spitting a glob of blood onto the floor. "I have no idea what you're so upset about." One more deep breath allowed him to stand erect, even though he still swayed on his feet slightly. "What do you mean she shot Max? Morgana was one of yours." His eyes searched Eli's.

"Well she's not anymore."

Samson's gaze swept over all of them. It wasn't until his eyes landed on Zoriana that he seemed to sense something. "Wasn't there another girl with you when you guys were here last time?"

No one said anything. The silence spoke for itself.

"Damn. I'm sorry. I didn't know. You have to believe I would have never sold anything to her if I knew..." His wild eyes swung between Eli and Zoriana, pleading. "We go way back. You know I would never betray you." His eyes zeroed in on Zoriana, his next statement meant only for her. "You know I would never do anything to hurt you." Even though it was clear he was still hurting from the damage that had been inflicted upon him, he limped towards Zoriana. "I'm sorry."

It was the last thing Willow could make out before he dropped his voice to whisper other things for only Zoriana to hear. It made her wonder about their past. Tears gathered in Zoriana's eyes as she listened to Samson. Once he finished, she stepped away from him without a word and left the building.

After they watched her leave, Eli approached Samson. "No hard feelings?" He extended his hand. All Willow could think was that if she'd just had her ass handed to her by people that were supposed to be her friends, they would be far from cool.

"Just the price of doing business, man." Samson shook Eli's hand while still massaging the tender wound on his side.

The only gestures of good faith he received from the other two, if you wanted to call it that, was a head nod from Max and a death glare from Phaedra. Samson knew not to push his luck. Samson's men were beginning to wake up from the spell they were placed under. Many shook their heads groggily and looked around in confusion. Willow stepped over one man as they exited the warehouse and returned to the RV. Zoriana was already sitting in the passenger seat staring vacantly through the windshield. This time Phaedra jumped into the driver's seat and drove them back to Walker House; the ride even quieter than when they set out.

CHAPTER 4

Eli

IT WAS ALREADY late afternoon of the next day when Eli decided he'd waited long enough to broach the difficult conversation with Zoriana about them adding new members to the Protectors. He was prepared for physical violence. Hopefully, it wouldn't come to that, but Zoriana's temper was so volatile lately, he wasn't sure what to expect.

He paced the floor of the training room as he waited for her to arrive. Phaedra had offered to be here, but he thought it best that it just be the two of them. Beyond being members of the Protectors, who'd sworn an oath to protect Willow and each other, they were also bound to each other as family. She was his aunt. He was her nephew. If he couldn't reach her through logic and reason, he wasn't above pulling on the familial heartstrings.

When she entered the room she seemed weary. Her guard was up.

"Thanks for coming."

"Didn't really seem like I had a choice." Her eyes bore into his like she was trying to read his thoughts before he could utter them.

"I won't drag this out..." He sighed. "We need to add new members to the Protectors now, so we can begin training them."

Her nostrils flared in anger and her face reddened. "We just buried her and already you're trying to replace her."

Before he had a chance to respond she'd used her magic to quickly pluck a staff off the wall. It reached her hands in seconds. She wasted no time in striking him with it.

"Baculum, veni ad me." After saying the words a staff appeared in his hands.

Maybe this was just what she needed to unleash some of the pent up anger that was waiting to go off like a lit powder keg.

"Why do you keep acting like everyone is the enemy?" He swung his staff at her, but she ducked, narrowly missing the sturdy, wooden stick. "You know I loved her too."

"You know nothing of a mother's love." The words came out through gritted teeth as she advanced on him, swinging the staff again and again, trying to back him against the wall. With each angry swipe, he dodged her.

"I know that." He was trying to take it easy on her because he knew she was grieving, but the way she was coming after him, its like she was out for blood. "It still doesn't mean I loved her any less or I don't care." In quick succession, he used a combination move to fake her out and then knocked her off her feet.

Zoriana panted, angry eyes glared at him from her seated position on the mat. He reached out a hand to pull her up, even though he knew she was like confronting a spitting, hissing cat at this point. He reminded her once again. "I'm not your enemy, aunt." He hoped the familial endearment would cool her temper. "We have a common enemy, and if we're going to defeat Killian and Morgana we're going to need all the help we can get... which is why we have to accept new people."

She didn't bat his hand away in anger or take his offered help. Silently, she rose to her feet. Her hand reached up and pulled a necklace from beneath her shirt. He recognized it as Mathilda's talisman. She clutched it in her hand.

Several charged seconds passed before she looked at him. Tears swam in her eyes, the despair dueling with her rage for dominance. "I don't know how to stop being angry?" The confession seemed to lift some of the burden she'd been carrying around. "When I let it take over, the hole in my heart doesn't seem so big. I don't feel like I want to go to bed and stay there indefinitely." Her lip trembled and she batted away the tear that had started to fall. "The sadness doesn't feel like this deep, dark, bottomless hole I've fallen into... so I keep wanting to hold onto the anger so I don't lose myself." The last words rushed out of her before she broke down weeping.

Eli pulled her into his arms and let her sob. He stroked her hair. "It's okay." He crooned the soothing words to her over and over. Unfortunately, Alistair, his uncle wasn't handling his grief that well either from what his parents had said. It was on the tip of his tongue to ask her if she'd talked with him about this, but he decided against it. "I'm sorry." It was the only other thing he could think to offer her.

After about ten minutes of crying into his shoulder, she pulled away and wiped her eyes. She looked at him with red-rimmed, puffy eyes and sniffled. "Do what's best for The Protectors... you won't get anymore pushback from me."

Before he could say anything else, she turned and left the room. He watched her leave without stopping her. After tidying up the room, he decided to pay his father a visit.

When he entered his parents' quarters, his mother greeted him. "It's good to see you." His mother gave him a hug. The embrace was longer and tighter than it normally was and he knew she must be thinking of Zoriana's loss and reminding herself that she still had her child. Would he one day understand that kind of fierce, unconditional love?

Hi mother released him. "Do you want something to eat or drink? I can whip up something in no time."

"Thank you, but I'm fine. I came to see father."

She paused, her eyes never leaving his. He was sure she'd already guessed his visit had to do with Protectors' business. "Promise me the two of you won't fight."

"I can't make a promise, but I will do my best not to. Does that work for you?" He offered her a small smile.

"I guess it will have to do... I always appreciated your honesty... even as a young boy, you never lied." She smiled at him and brushed his hair off his forehead. "Your father is in his office."

He left her and went to his father's home office. Before he knocked on the door, he inhaled and then let out a quick breath, readying himself for the encounter with his father. For his mother's sake, he would not let things get heated between them. He knocked twice.

"Come in." His father's voice called out on the other side of the door.

He pushed the door open and stepped inside. Neither of them said anything. They just regarded each other for several seconds. Finally, he came in and shut the door behind him. He took a seat in front of the desk before he started talking. "We're planning to move forward in adding members to the Protectors to make up for the ones we've lost."

"Clearly, you're not looking for my or the Council's approval or you'd be coming here to ask permission."

Is he trying to goad me into an argument?

He chose not to react to his father's statement.

If Willow could turn over a new leaf by embracing her training, then he could definitely avoid arguing with his father. "We have to replenish our numbers if we're going to defeat Killian and also take down Morgana." The logical explanation should be enough to make his father see reason.

They regarded each other for a moment, again neither of them speaking. His father must have been surprised that he didn't bristle or instantly anger over his comment.

"Yes, we do need to bring on new members... it makes sense." Barely a few seconds had passed before a sly grin passed across his father's face. He was instantly on high alert. "Why isn't Phaedra here discussing this with me? After all, she is the leader of the Protectors. The Council hasn't yet reinstated you to that position."

In an involuntary reaction that was beyond his control, his lip twitched. It took an iron will not to react to his father's vindictive tone. Well, the joke was on him; he wouldn't give him the satisfaction. Keeping his face neutral, he responded. "You're right. I haven't been reinstated...yet. I will come back with Phaedra this afternoon." He stood and walked to the door. Before he could leave, his father called out to him. "There's no need for you to come back with Phaedra. She and I should be able to discuss things."

Eli bit the inside of his cheek and gripped the doorknob. He was about to lose this game. It was hard, but he swallowed down his anger and nearly choked on it when he answered without turning to face him. "I'll see to it she comes alone." He opened the door and left abruptly.

Minutes later, he was knocking on Phaedra's door. The instant she opened the door, he breezed past her.

"I didn't react to that smug bastard. I didn't let him get the better of me." He paced the floor back and forth, mostly talking to himself. The anger he'd held in check during his father's taunting flared to the surface. "He tried."

"Who are you talking about?" Phaedra shut the door.

"My father."

When he finally turned around to face her, he noticed they weren't alone. He shouldn't have been surprised. Usually wherever you found Phaedra these days, Max was there.

"Hey Max."

"Hey." Max gave a wave. He wore his usual surfer dude attire.

"What are you doing here?" Phaedra crossed her arms over her chest waiting for an answer.

"I just came from my father. He wants to speak with the leader about adding new members." He rolled his eyes and plopped down on the couch next to Max.

"Zoriana's okay with this?" The skeptical look on her face as she narrowed her eyes at him wasn't subtle in the least.

"Yeah, things went fine." He didn't look at her when he replied.

"You're lying."

"Okay they didn't go fine. We ended up fighting for a while, but eventually they were fine and she signed off on new members. Happy." He didn't know which was worse, being scolded by Phaedra or his mother.

"Yes."

At least she didn't gloat.

"I'll go and speak with your father shortly. I'm sure he'll have some opinions about who should be on the short list to join the Protectors."

"I'm sure he will, which is why we need to create our own list before you go in to see him."

"Agreed." She walked over to desk and retrieved a notepad and pencil. "Let's brainstorm. Max, you can help."

She sat down in an armchair and began scribbling on the pad.

"Whatever you need, babe." He leaned forward with a smirk on his face.

It took a strong, confident man to deal with Phaedra's take-charge attitude. Many of the men who were part of the coven or from other covens had tried for a few years to be her companion, but most of them never stuck. Most of them had been insecure in their own manhood to appreciate her. He was glad that Max not only appreciated this quality, he loved this about her.

The three of them quickly got to work and in forty-five minutes had compiled a list of the top people that The Council couldn't say no to. More importantly, that his father couldn't say no to.

"I better get going. Make sure Willow hasn't gotten herself into trouble or anything."

"I'll let you know how the meeting goes when I finish talking to him." She followed him to the door with the list in her hands.

"Okay. Later." He stuffed his hands into the pockets of his jeans and walked to his apartment. Maybe Willow would be up for more training... or for something else. His mind skipped over training and went to the wicked, lusty thoughts his mind suddenly conjured up. It had been a while and right now all he could think of was taking her in a few different positions before the night was over.

"Willow?" He called out when he entered the apartment. "Are you here?" She must have been in the bedroom. The minute he opened the door, his eyes landed on her. Sweaty and unconscious, she thrashed around on the bed in the grips of some horrendous nightmare. He rushed to her side and tried to shake her awake. "Willow! Willow! Wake up." How long had she been like this?

The last time this had happened he had been terrified. Fear once again seized him. The bloody nose that began told him whatever was happening in the dream was getting worse.

"Willow! Please! Wake up!" The plea fell on deaf ears as he shook her once again.

CHAPTER 5

Willow

IF SHE'D KNOWN her nap would result in an encounter with Killian, she would have tried her best to stay awake. This time when he tried to grab her, she'd fought back. The first blast of energy she'd given him had sent him flying backwards. The murderous look he sported when he'd regained his composure should have terrified her, but it gave her confidence. When some of his minions rushed forward to try and take hold of her, she'd been able to blast them backwards at an even greater distance, even knocking one unconscious. Unfortunately, she was no match for Killian and Katana combined.

When Katana's steel fingers clamped themselves on her biceps, holding her in place, she squirmed and wiggled to no avail. Killian stalked towards her, ready to do God knows what to her in retaliation. She tried to rear back and slam the back of her head into Katana's face like she'd seen in the movies. The only thing she got for her efforts was a stinging pain when her head collided with her nose and Katana's villainous laughter filling her ears.

"Someone is doing her best to fight back. It's cute. Like a little bird." Her hands squeezed her arms tighter, making Willow wince in pain.

Killian strode toward them and stopped in front of her, his face mere inches from hers. The thunderous look that he'd sported moments ago dropped away and he gave her a wicked grin. "Yes..." He hissed. "It is rather cute when you fight back." His hand caressed her face while his eyes penetrated hers, trying to pluck her thoughts from them. She glared back at him. There was no way she would give him the satisfaction of cowering in fear. Let him do what he was going to do, she'd take it.

When it was clear he wasn't going to get the reaction he wanted, he grabbed her head between his hands as he'd done before and tried to extract what he wanted to know. She fought with all her might to stay silent and not let the screams that wailed in her head come out of her mouth. Her hands dangled by her side, her body like a limp noodle. The tears ran silently and blood dripped from her nose onto her shirt as her mind resisted him and she willed her arm to respond. After many agonizing seconds, her arm twitched in awareness. Slowly, she raised it until her fingers grazed the starched, white dress shirt he wore and she immediately shot a blast of energy into his chest before he could stop her. It caught him off guard again and he flew a few feet back.

She gathered what energy she could and said with force, "Wake up." Right after she said the words her eyes opened and she found herself being shaken by a distraught Eli.

The minute he realized she was awake, he hugged her to his chest without saying anything. She'd seen the panic on his face. She knew how powerless he felt that he couldn't stop Killian from coming into her dreams. All he could do was try and wake her up. She wrapped her arms about him and held him tightly.

A few minutes passed before he whispered into her hair. "Are you okay?"

"My head hurts, but I'm okay."

He eased his hold on her and pulled back to look at her face. "You promise?"

She nodded and grinned at him despite the pounding in her head. "I fought back this time. I wasn't scared."

"You did?" He gave her a smile that exposed his teeth and lit up his eyes. It made her heart soar.

"Yeah. I blasted him twice with my faery energy... wish you could have been there to see it."

"That's my girl." His grin got even bigger if that was possible.

Headache be damned, having Eli be proud of her meant the world to her. Yeah, she knew she didn't need validation from her, but she knew what a pain she'd been to train and seeing the look of awe and satisfaction light up his face gave her a warm feeling inside.

He hugged her to his body once more. "I'm so proud of you."

***

Knowing that she hadn't wanted to try and go back to sleep right away, he'd carried her into the bathroom and ran a bath. As the tub filled, he'd helped her clean her face. When he stripped them both naked and settled them in the tub she hadn't protested. It felt so nice to be seated between his thighs, leaning back onto his chest. The lavender he'd scented the water with wafted up and relaxed her. He kissed her temple and she sighed with deep contentment. There was no place else she wanted to be in that moment. No one else she'd rather be with.

It wasn't long before she was humming. She found herself humming a familiar tune. The Cure's 'Lovesong' began to take shape as his hands rubbed and massaged her body, making her feel boneless and replete, cared for and loved. Soon, she could feel his nose and then his lips against the skin of her collarbone.

"Have I ever told you how beautiful your voice is even when you're just humming?" He dusted her skin with feather light kisses. The effect his touch and his words had on her was like a drug. They made her soft and compliant. His next words brought her out of the lull. "Do you still think of the life you could have had if I hadn't sabotaged it?" The plea hidden in his words touched her heart. After everything that had happened, he still sought her forgiveness. His hands seemed to grip her tighter, like he somehow expected her to flee and escape him for his crime.

She sat in the circle of his embrace, the sudsy water cloaking them, and pondered his question. "Sometimes when I'm able to find the time to play, my fingers will be plucking and strumming chords on my guitar and I think about being on stage..." She caressed his arm. "I rather like singing for an audience of one these days." She rubbed her cheek against his forearm that held her tight.

He let out the breath he'd been holding while he waited for her answer. "Will you sing for me?" The request was spoken into her skin as he pressed his lips to all the right places.

The words of the song echoed off the tiles of the bathroom walls as she sang. Strong arms wrapped around her and held her securely as if he was trying to become part of her. His cheek pressed against her back and every now and then he rubbed his stubbled jaw against her wet skin, sending a sweet sensation rippling through her body. She continued to sing while he held her and caressed her. The headache that had persisted after her encounter with Killian slowly receded. She would have stayed like that with him until the water was ice cold, but fifteen minutes later he pulled her from the bathtub. He'd barely dried her skin with the towel before he guided her back into the bedroom and onto the bed. Their slick, damp skin glided against each other as he covered her body with his. She yielded to him. It had been weeks since their lovemaking was romantic and not just simply the two of them going through the motions to satisfy their needs.

There was no verbal communication needed as he took her. Their eyes held each other's gaze as he breached her walls, pushing his cock deep inside of her, scalding her with his heat. When he struck a spot that made her want to scream the roof down, his mouth descended on hers to take her cries and soft pleas.

Her nails raked his back when his thrusts became deeper and slower. When he pulled back to stare at her, his eyes trapping her in place, she knew she was going to unravel in the most delicious way possible. His cock was marking each place it touched inside of her.

He grabbed her hands and held her wrists securely above her head while he plowed into her, never taking his eyes from hers. It was the sexiest thing. He sped up the pace, but still plunged deeply. She couldn't stop her mouth from dropping open in an 'O' of ecstasy. He must have sensed she was on the verge of climaxing because he buried his face in the crook of her neck, but still continued to hold her immobile while pounding into her. All too soon she was coming. She bit his shoulder and came hard. A minute later, he followed her. He emptied himself inside of her, her honeyed walls milking him of every drop.

Their combined release coated her thighs. His lips kissed the sweat-dampened skin of her neck and shoulders. They hadn't used a condom. It was the first time that ever happened. Usually, they were always so careful. She knew she should be worried or upset that they'd forgotten or been careless, but she wasn't.

Slowly, he pulled out of her and slid down her body until his head was nestled on her chest. Her thighs still cradled him and he wrapped his arms around her, snuggling into her body. Sleep was pulling at every part of her. She stroked his hair. It comforted her to know that he couldn't bare to part from her either. Lazily, she rubbed his back as her eyes drooped with drowsiness.

Before she fell asleep, she told him what had been on her mind before the nightmare with Killian. "Tomorrow, I want you to help me find a faery to teach me how to use my gifts."

If he had a reaction or responded she didn't know because she was out the minute the last word left her lips.

***

The next morning they sat in the library going through some of the faery books again.

"Why couldn't I have inherited a more badass fae ability, like shapeshifting or flying or something? What the hell is faery dust good for? What can I do with it?" It was hard not to whine about her lack of faery skills.

Eli shut the book he'd been looking at. For a moment, he opened his mouth like he was going to say something then he shut it.

"What?"

"I'm going to say something, but you're not going to like it."

Her curiosity was getting the better of her now. She leaned forward on the table. "Just say it."

"Cora."

The second her name left his lips she slammed back in her seat; crossed her arms over her chest and shook her head vehemently. "No."

"Listen, I know you're still mad at her over what happened with me, which I appreciate..." He took her hand in his, "But…" At the word 'but,' she tried to pull her hand away. He kept a hold on it. "If you're serious about really learning your fae abilities, you'll let Cora help you. I'm sure she can reach out to find someone to help you. It's what you said you wanted last night, right?"

She was trying to block him out, but he squeezed her hand. Eventually, she relented and took a look at him, but the scowl didn't leave her face.

"Everyone answers to someone, Willow. I know you think she could have stopped what happened to me, but she couldn't. She's beholden to the Congress of Supernatural Beings like everyone else. She's not above the law, so cut the old woman a break, okay? For me?" He gave her one of his brilliant smiles.

She wanted to stay mad, but she couldn't. Not when he looked at her like that. "For you, I will go talk to her."

A huge grin broke out across his face and he came around the table and began to pepper her face with kisses. She couldn't help giggling. "Stop. Enid's going to see us."

He snorted and continued, "I'm sure she's seen all kinds of things. I doubt us kissing is going to bother her."

"What if she has a heart attack?" She was trying to play devil's advocate, but if she was honest, his kisses were making her want to do naughty things in the stacks of books.

He guffawed, "Enid's had a long life."

This sent her off into peals of laughter and she allowed him to pull her from her seat and guide her into the stacks.

After a quick romp, they both walked out of the stacks and adjusted their clothing.

"You have to come with me to see Cora. I don't trust myself not to be rude to her.

"Fine."

CHAPTER 6

Eli

THE LAST TIME he'd seen Cora was at The Council meeting. It had been surprising to see her there that day, because when they returned from Egypt they'd been told her health was once again on the decline. She hadn't even been able to attend Mathilda's funeral.

When Willow had been summoned to visit her during their previous stay at the coven, he'd never entered the room. In fact, it had been years since he'd stepped foot into the chamber, probably since he was a boy.

After knocking, the door swung open to permit them. Cora was propped up against a myriad of pillows, looking like a wrinkled, old doll in her pristine, white nightgown.

"I was wondering when you two would pay me a visit."

As they walked across the huge bedroom towards her, he wondered if she'd been anticipating their visit because a lone chair sat beside the bed. Despite her current feelings towards Cora, Willow sat on the edge of the bed and let him take the chair.

"How are you?" He looked her over, expecting to see something that would indicate the depth of her ill health.

"Right as rain, child." She looked between the two of them.

Willow wasn't looking at her. She appeared to be sulking again. He nudged her. "Willow has something she wants to ask you about."

She gave him a dirty look before turning a false smile on Cora. "Eli thought it might be a good idea to come here and ask you about..."

"I have some things I must tell you both." Cora interrupted her before a wracking cough shook her body for several seconds. Eli reached for the pitcher of water and poured a glass. Willow took it from his hands and helped Cora to drink a little.

"Thank you, my dear." Cora said regally, like a queen, once Willow removed the glass from her lips. "As I was saying, I have some things to tell you both."

Willow looked over at him, and he shrugged his shoulders at her. He had no idea what Cora needed to tell them. He'd simply wanted her to come so Cora could help her find a faery that could mentor her.

She looked between the two of them. "When your mother visited the coven before her death she spoke of the two of you. Of course, Eli heard part of that since he snuck into the room." She looked pointedly at him and glanced back at Willow. "After he was made to leave the room, Hyacinth told the Council of Elders that you and Eli would fall in love and marry."

To say he was shocked would be a huge understatement. Willow kept her eyes trained on Cora, although he was looking at her. It was hard to gauge her reaction since she was so focused on the old woman.

"The Elders kept this from you because they hoped her prophecy wouldn't come true." Cora redirected her attention back to him. "When the Congress of Supernatural Beings found out Killian's intent for Hyacinth and her bloodline, they enacted the law regarding love and marriage with the Oracle. It was to deter any other supernatural factions from having the idea to use the Oracle's powers for their own gain."

He was struck speechless by everything she was saying.

Cora reached over and took each of their hands in one of hers. "They knew they had to keep you on as one of her Protectors so that she would be safe, because in all of Hyacinth's visions there was never a scenario where Willow survived without you. But it was also why it was forbidden for you to interact with her. If you never engaged with her then maybe Hyacinth's prophecy wouldn't come true, and then the coven wouldn't have to worry we might have a target painted on our backs if someone believed we might be trying to use the Oracle's powers for our own gain."

So many things became clear. Cora must have noticed the recognition that crossed his face.

"It was why the punishment had to be swift and harsh when you crossed that line. We had to demonstrate to Congress that we didn't condone the relationship, that we weren't looking to use Willow for our own benefit."

Willow still had yet to say anything. What was going on in that head of hers?

"Do you understand, child?" Her question was directed at Willow.

It was several moments before Willow spoke. Her voice was eerily calm, "All of this is because of him. It's always because of Killian. I want him out of my life. I'm sick and tired of it. I've yet to meet him and so much of my life is dictated by his very existence."

Cora looked over Willow's shoulder at him.

"We're going to get him... and then you won't have to worry about him anymore. I promise." He hoped that she believed that they could do this. Now was not the time for her to doubt or get defeated.

She continued speaking like she hadn't heard him. "It doesn't help that not only does he have Morgana that knew our plans, but they now have the Book of Prophecy. What if there's something in there that Killian and Morgana have figured out they can use against us?"

He was about to interject when Cora beat him to it.

"They can't child." Her tone seemed so sure.

"How do you know that?" Willow's question was filled with skepticism, and he didn't try to hide that he felt the same way. There was no way that she could know that. Willow was right. The deck was stacked against them.

"Because she doesn't have the key." Cora's statement hung in the air.

"How would you know that?

"What are you talking about? What key?" Both he and Willow lobbed questions at her at the same time. Things were getting weird.

"You need a key to open the book."

Some people loved wielding secrets and lording them over others. If Cora were one of those people, she would be sporting a smug look right about now, and he would have gladly slapped it off her face. Instead she looked contrite. A look he'd never seen on her face before, not even when she stripped him of his hereditary powers. Sure she said how sorry she was, but anyone can say things, doesn't mean they actually mean them. This time she looked sincerely apologetic. Willow looked ready to shake the frail, old woman if she didn't answer.

"Before you left here the last time and I gave you the letters..."

"Yes..." Suspicion clung to the word and Willow narrowed her gaze. "What didn't you tell me?"

His eyes volleyed between the two women. What exactly happened during that visit?

"I asked you about your necklace." Cora's eyes went to the necklace in question. The one he knew that Willow very rarely, if ever took off.

Her hand flew up to her throat and grasped the snake pendant between her fingers. "What about my necklace?"

"It's the key. It opens the Book of Prophecy. It will only work for you because you're an Oracle. Killian and Morgana must have you and the necklace, the key to open the book."

The surprises just kept on coming today. Willow seemed to be just as stunned as he was. Her mouth kept opening and closing, but no words came out. Once again, Cora stated what was on his mind before he could voice the question aloud.

"I didn't want to reveal that before you left in case anything went wrong and that information fell into the wrong hands."

"How did you come to know that?" Willow's glance alternated between the necklace and Cora.

He couldn't take his eyes off the necklace. Back in Egypt, he never had the opportunity to see the book once Willow found it and before Morgana stole it. She never mentioned a keyhole or anything that the necklace would have slipped into. How exactly did it open the book? Cora hadn't even had the opportunity to answer Willow's latest question, but he couldn't keep himself from asking the thought that was rolling around in his head. "How does the necklace open the book?"

"One question at a time." She reprimanded him. "During your mother's stay with us, she had a vision about the necklace and came to me in the middle of the night. After she told me what she'd seen, she forbid me to write it down and didn't want to put it in her letters to you. Again, she was concerned the information would fall into the wrong hands." Cora looked at Willow searching for understanding.

"And what if you'd died before you could tell me?"

If the situation weren't so serious he might have laughed out loud. Cora beat him to it. The old woman cackled with an energy he didn't think her brittle bones were still capable of.

"Don't worry child, I would have made sure the information was passed on securely to you. After all, that's what magic is for." She giggled some more and took a deep breath. "As for your question about how the key opens the book... that part Hyacinth did not disclose to me. She simply said that when the time came all would be revealed."

The gears in Willow's head were turning as she fondled the necklace. So much information has been dumped on them. At some point they would need to share with the others, but his brain was still trying to process everything.

"My dears, I'm getting very tired. That's enough for today." Cora gave a demure yawn and lay back against the pillows.

Willow stood up and headed for the door. Eli looked at her back with a shocked, perplexed look and back to a sleeping Cora. He stood and followed Willow with an incredulous look on his face. "That's it. You're not going to make sure she's told us everything?"

Willow kept walking to the bedroom door. "Nope." She didn't seem the least bit fazed by the abrupt end to the conversation.

Eli hurried to keep up with her, but looked at the bed over his shoulder. "Really?"

"Nope. I've learned that when Cora is done with something, you just have to wait. There is no getting her to talk before she's ready. 'Sometimes things need to come in steps and stages of what we can handle and how soon we can handle it.'" Clearly, Cora had uttered those words to her before. "If she has more, she'll summon us when she's ready."

They exited the bedroom.

"Stop." Eli halted in his steps and Willow turned to face him. He couldn't read her expression.

"Are you okay? We just got a truckload of information dumped on us in there and you haven't really said anything." He peered at her face. "Should I be concerned?"

"I'm fine." Her face was still passive.

He wasn't sure whether to believe her or not, but so far, Willow had never lied to him.

"Okay." Now wasn't the time to start an argument. If she said she was fine then he would leave it at that. Right now they needed to talk this through and figure out if and when and what they would share with the group. There was still so much to be done. He wondered if Phaedra had had the opportunity to speak with his father about the new candidates they wanted to bring on. Plus, there was still the matter of Willow's training. As they walked away from Cora's bedchamber, he realized that Willow never got to ask her about ideas for a faery mentor.

CHAPTER 7

Willow

ON THE INSIDE, she was freaking out. She wasn't quite sure which news was freaking her out more: hearing about her mother's prophecy regarding her and Eli falling in love and getting married, how the Congress of Supernatural Beings was so sure she was going to give her powers to the first group that showed her a little love and attention or that she'd been wearing the key this whole damn time. The more Cora had unloaded one secret after the other, she'd been unsure whether she should laugh, cry or be pissed off.

The beginnings of a migraine were coming on and she had to resist the urge to rub her temples. All she did know was that Killian was the cause of so much of the stress and crazy in her life, and the sooner they got rid of him the better. She wanted her life back and she wanted to live her life on her own terms, not have it decided by someone else.

An idea started to take shape in her mind as they walked back to Eli's apartment. If she could get Eli to agree to it, they might stand a chance against Killian and Morgana. Sometimes you had to fight just as dirty as the enemy if you were going to be victorious.

"I think I have an idea." Her fingers tied themselves in knots as she anxiously fidgeted while getting situated on the couch. She was nervous and unsure about what he would think.

"Okay." He grabbed two bottles of water from the refrigerator and handed her one as he took a seat beside her on the sofa.

She watched him take a swig of his water before she spoke. "Remember the conversation we had in the RV about the different types of magic?

He nodded, still not understanding where she was headed with her line of questioning. "Yeah."

"Well, I was thinking..." She studied his face carefully as she said her next words. "You said that people could be students of magic by studying and training." She quickened her pace and rushed out her next words. "We're already going to be doing all of the other training so why don't you teach me how to become a witch?" She looked at him with a hopeful expression and licked her suddenly dry lips. It was unclear how he felt about what she'd just suggested or what he was going to say. It took him a long time to say anything. "What do you think?" Now she was apprehensive. Her smile faltered.

"I don't know... Do you think it's the right choice to make right now? If you remember we were originally going to see Cora because you wanted to get a faery to train you in your fae abilities and now on top of all that you want to add being a witch too?"

When he said it like that, he made her second guess herself and she didn't like the feeling. "Well when you put it like that, it sounds like a bad idea." She didn't even try to keep the hurt from coming through in her words.

"Willow, I'm not trying to be a dick, but it just seems like a lot. You still have so much to learn now as it is." His voice sounded so weary of her idea.

She didn't want him to say no before he actually gave it some real consideration and thought. "But don't you see that magic may be what I'll need to help defeat them." She tried to reason with him. "The more skills, tools and tricks I have up my sleeve the better prepared I'll be to face him.

"Haven't you ever heard the expression: jack of all trades, master of none?"

Wow! Is that what he thinks of me? "So you don't believe that I'm capable of learning everything?" Even as the words left her mouth, she knew her track record hadn't been that great at sticking to learning and training, but she was determined to prove him wrong.

"I didn't say I didn't believe in you." He reached for her hand, but she moved it out of his reach. "I'm just saying that's a lot to take on..." His eyes roamed over her face. "But... if you really think it will be beneficial to you... I'll teach you."

"Really?" She clapped her hands together. She went to throw her arms around his neck, but he stopped her.

"But you have to be super serious about this, Willow." Eli spoke in his stern tone of voice he sometimes took with her when he was training her, trying to show her he meant business.

"I know, I know. I will." She bounced up and down before finally getting her arms around his neck and showering his face with kisses.

"I mean it. The first time there is any goofing off, you're not serious or I get any pushback I'm ending it." He was still trying to be stern, but she could feel him succumbing to her kisses. After a few more seconds Eli extricated himself from her arms. "I'm going to go call Phaedra and tell her we need to meet. The sooner we relay everything that Cora told us and find out who my father okayed to join the Protectors the sooner we can start making a plan."

Yes, they certainly needed a plan, but they also needed to know where Killian was located. She'd had a glimpse of the wooded area surrounding his castle, but she still had no idea where it was located. If they were lucky, hopefully she'd have another vision soon that would show her exactly where they could find him.

After he left the room to make the call the smile fell away. She felt a little guilty about leaving out the other part of her idea. It was just that she had expected him to jump all over the idea for her to learn magic and when he had resisted, she knew she needed to broach the rest of what she was considering to the group as a whole. She didn't want him nixing it. The others might even help persuade him. If he was outvoted then he wouldn't be able to say no.

***

When they arrived to the training room, Max and Phaedra were already there. Zoriana arrived only a few minutes after them.

"First things first, what did my father have to say about our list of candidates?"

Phaedra handed over the list they'd compiled earlier. "Just like we thought. He vetoed the people we knew he would and okayed the ones we hoped he would after seeing those people. It's a good thing your father is so predictable."

Eli sported a grin as he read through the list of candidates that had received his father's seal of approval.

This was good. If Eli was in a good mood before she made her suggestion to the group then everything might just go well.

Eli tried to pass the list to Zoriana, but she declined. "I trust you guys will choose the right people to..." She stopped herself from saying something. "I trust you."

Willow started talking to cover the awkwardness. "One of the reasons we called you guys here is because we just had an illuminating conversation with Cora." That comment got everyone's attention.

Between her and Eli they relayed all the information that Cora had shared. Thankfully, no one interrupted as they told the story. Many of their facial expressions had changed to shock and surprise at the same moments as her and Eli when they'd heard everything for the first time. When they finished no one spoke for the first few moments. It was evident that they were trying to process all of the new information, the same way they had done.

"So can I be like your maid of honor at the wedding, but instead we call it dude of honor?" Max asked Willow, as he looked between her and Eli.

Phaedra slapped his arm in annoyance. "That's the one thing you pulled out of all of that?"

Zoriana and Eli also gave Max irritated glances, but she couldn't help the small smile that curled her lip. *Good ole Max.*

"There's more." She blurted, pulling everyone's attention. "Eli's agreed to teach me how to be a witch." Her eyes darted around at everyone, but before they could say anything she launched into the piece she'd left out of her conversation with Eli. "While he's training me, I think we all need to learn some black magic so we'll be formidable when we face down Killian and Morgana." She'd just dropped a major bomb, no, nuclear missile and was waiting for it to detonate. It still remained unclear just how catastrophic the fallout was going to be as she anxiously waited for one of them to speak.

She tried her best not to look at Eli. Anger was rolling off of him so strongly, for a split second she felt fearful.

"Are you out of your mind?" Phaedra exploded. "Mathilda was the last one to speak about black magic and look where that got her."

Out of the corner of her eye, she saw Zoriana flinch slightly over hearing Mathilda's name.

Max pleaded with her a little more calmly, "Willow, I've never known you to have a death wish... why would you even suggest such a thing." The disappointment rang threw loud and clear in his words. She avoided looking at his face, not wanting to see it written there too.

"Leave us." Eli's voice was a band of steel and everyone in that moment knew that to disobey it would be at their own peril. He was beyond angry with her, but at least he had the decency to force everyone to leave before he tore into her.

Once the door closed on them, several charged seconds ticked by without him saying a word. Finally, she worked up the nerve to look at him. The thunderous expression he wore looked like he was ready to commit violence. She swallowed, but stood her ground. "I think it will give us an advantage over Killian and Morgana if we..."

"Stop talking." His voice was still eerily calm, but she heard the edge to it, waiting to snap and eviscerate her. "Why didn't you share your idea with me?"

She opened her mouth to respond and he kept talking. "I'll tell you why, because you knew what I would say."

"I'm sorry."

"Don't Willow. You knew what you were doing. What were you thinking? Were you hoping to win them to your side and then I would have to go along with it?"

Her eyes dropped to the floor when he landed right on the truth of her plan. Recognition spread across his face. "That's exactly what you hoped." He shook his head and a bitter laugh fell from his lips. "It was thoughtless and careless of you to bring up using black magic in front of Zoriana when her parents and daughter were killed by it."

There was a part of her that felt contrite at his words, but the part of her that was fighting for survival said that it was for this very reason that they needed to learn it. If some of the witches had known black magic then, would Mathilda be dead? Would maybe one or both of Zoriana's parents still be alive?

Unfortunately, if she brought up that line of reasoning right now she was afraid that Eli's head would explode. While she'd been lost in her thoughts, it was clear that he had been also.

"I don't know if teaching you how to be a witch anymore is the best idea." The grim expression he held made her realize this had gone far worse than she imagined it would. He had to teach her.

"Look, I'm sorry. Please don't reconsider what you've already agreed to. I need to learn everything I can… please." She stepped towards him and tried to touch him, but he stepped away from her touch. He hung his head unable or unwilling to look at her, she wasn't sure.

His steps kept retreating backwards. "I'll think about it, but… I'm gonna go…" He never lifted his head to look at her before he turned and left the room.

Couldn't any of them understand that she just wanted to beat Killian and Morgana. She just wanted all of them to survive. She wasn't ready to give up yet. Zoriana was the only one that hadn't called her crazy. Maybe, just maybe, she could crack Zoriana.

CHAPTER 8

Eli

A COUPLE OF weeks had passed since Willow had gotten the bright idea that they needed to learn black magic in order to defeat Killian and Morgana. Although she'd dropped it, things had still been strained between them. He'd never seen her work harder at training, whether it was honing her hand-to-hand combat skills, her skills with the dagger or staff, Oracle abilities and even learning spells and potions, she'd become an exemplary student. It had taken him a few days after the incident to come around on teaching her how to be a witch. They all took turns on teaching her, because he and Phaedra also had their hands full dealing with the new recruits, Delaney and Evelyn, who went by Evie.

The other new addition to the training was Willow's fairy mentor. After they went back to Cora to get ask her for a recommendation, a day later, he'd shown up. His name was Cosmo Bitterjewel. His long, snow-white hair he wore in a braid down his back. He often showed up looking like the lead singer of a rock band: tight leather pants and shirts with half the buttons undone, when he chose to wear a shirt at all. Phaedra instantly took a disliking to him. He was still on the fence. Willow seemed to be learning a lot from him.

His gaze wandered over to the two of them working together in the corner of the large room. Cosmo must have said something funny because she was laughing. Quickly, he averted his gaze. He wasn't the jealous type and he certainly wasn't going to start acting like a jealous boyfriend now.

"Let's go Delaney, you're moving as slow as Archie out there. Pick up the pace. You have to be quicker than that. That's why Evie keeps beating you in every match." He walked over and took the staff out of his hand. Expertly he wielded the wooden stick, twirling it and swinging it in rapid-fire movements. "See? You have to become more coordinated and fluid in your movements." He tossed the staff back to Delaney. "Again."

As he stepped away, he couldn't help glancing in their direction one more time.

"You know that Willow would never cheat on you."

Startled, he looked up to find max standing nearby. "Who said I was worried?" He bristled at being read so easily.

Max chuckled. "Okay. That's why you keep looking over there every five seconds."

He wasn't worried about Willow cheating, he really wasn't. Its just things between them hadn't been right and he wasn't sure how to fix it. He wasn't going to tell Max this. The two of them were close, but this was their business. Max must have taken the hint that he wasn't in the mood for any more conversation because after a few minutes he walked off.

"That's enough sparring for today. Let's move over to the other room to practice spells and potions." He called out.

As he cleaned up and put things away, Phaedra came up beside him. "We've been training for two weeks now. The new members are..." He knew what she was thinking when she paused to find the right words. He was thinking it too. They would never be the perfect fit. She didn't complete her thought, but continued on. "What is the plan for when training is finished? We still have no idea where they are. Has Willow had any visions?"

"No." He didn't want to tell her that he wasn't exactly Willow's favorite person lately and wasn't sure that she would still confide in him the way she had before. That was his own insecurity that he would keep to himself. "If she comes up with something you know I'll let you know immediately." He finally met her gaze. "Until then we keep training."

Phaedra simply nodded and left to head to the other room. It felt like everyone was on edge lately. They were training for a battle and had no idea when it would come or where it would be fought. Everyone was frustrated. The only ones that didn't seem phased by it all were Evie and Delaney. Not to say they didn't know what was at stake, they simply hadn't lived through it all like the rest of them had.

"You did well today." Cosmo heaped on the praise as they walked towards him.

"Thanks. I feel like I'm really getting better at so many of my fae abilities now that we've been training together." Willow gave Cosmo a quick hug and walked away. She gathered her things and finally acknowledged he was even in the room. "Hey, I'm going to head over and get set up. I think I'm mixing a wrong ingredient into my latest potion and Evie said she would give me a hand."

"Okay. I'll meet you there." He watched her walk out of the room. When he looked up, he noticed he wasn't the only one watching her leave. He gave the faery a hard stare.

Cosmo caught the glare and angry vibes and began to chuckle. This only irritated Eli further. "Wait..." Cosmo smirked and chuckled. "You're getting the wrong idea." He shook his head and walked towards Eli. "I have no interest in Willow like that. It's purely platonic."

Eli wasn't sure whether he should believe him or not.

"It's true. I'm just a fan because of her abilities. Her enthusiasm for learning is ridiculous. There is a lot of untapped potential there. She may only be half fae, but..." Cosmo looed back towards the door that Willow had left through before he turned back to Eli. "It's thrilling for an old faery like me that hasn't trained anyone in a while. I'm like a Jedi master, Obi-Wan and she's like Luke Skywalker."

To look at Cosmo you wouldn't think he was a day over twenty-five. *Fuckin' faeries.* They barely aged. He was probably two hundred years old or more.

Eli let go of his anger, so much for not being the jealous boyfriend. "I'm sorry." He offered Cosmo. "I really appreciate you training her... everyone's just been a little on edge..."

"Yeah, I know." Cosmo grew serious. "She told me about you guys losing a member of your team and the whole saga of Killian and Morgana. Some pretty heavy stuff you guys are dealing with."

For some reason, Cosmo's laidback attitude had reminded him of Max, but when he'd grown serious, as he was now, he was reminded of Ulrik. Even though he hadn't been in their lives that long he had left an impact because of his compassionate nature. From time to time, like now, something would happen and remind him of the Viking vampire.

"You have this weird look on your face. Everything okay?" Cosmo looked at him with concern.

"Yeah, I'm fine... You just reminded me of someone." An awkward silence settled between them.

"Well I better get going." Cosmo grabbed his things and left.

Eli nodded and went back to cleaning up the room. The sound of the door opening and swinging shut let him know when Cosmo left.

In the quiet and stillness of the room, without the constant motion of activity or training to keep the thoughts at bay, he wondered when this would all be over. Would their fights ever get to be about something normal and not whether she should be trying to save her life by using black magic?

He finished putting everything away and left to join the others.

CHAPTER 9

Willow

"I'M MEETING UP with Evie to go over some spells. I'll be back in a bit." The lie she'd just told rolled so easily off her tongue, it scared her a bit. She hated lying to him. She hated the way things had been between them lately. Everyday she wanted to fix it, but she knew as long as they both stood on opposite sides of the black magic debate this void might always be there between them.

After she closed the door and walked down the corridor she tried to push the troubling thought away. It wasn't Evie she was heading to see. She'd finally worked up the nerve to confront Zoriana and see if she would change her mind. The woman had proved elusive and hard to pen down. It had taken her some time, but she'd finally learned her habits and knew exactly where she'd be right now that would afford them some privacy.

Willow crept down the hall, looking this way and that, worried she would run into one of the other Protectors that might innocently tell Eli they saw her tonight, in a place other than where she said she was going. She slipped into shadows and looked out from corners until she arrived at the kitchens, where she knew Zoriana would be.

The Walker House was like living on a college campus. Everyone had their own apartments, but there were also common areas like dining halls, the kitchens, and the library, that you shared with everyone else. Usually at this hour the kitchens were dead. She was almost guaranteed that her conversation with Zoriana would be private.

The minute she stepped into Zoriana's line of sight and the woman recognized her; things became tense.

"Are you following me?" She looked around wildly. "How did you know I'd be here?" Her defenses were up as she scooted the chair back against the cobblestoned floor.

Willow slowly slid into the seat across from her. "No one knows I'm here and I'd like to keep it that way." The tone of her voice sounded like she was trying to soothe a wild horse that didn't want to go back into the pen. "I just want to talk."

Zoriana remained seated, but she didn't try and drag her chair closer to the table. "What do you want?" Her eyes still skittered around the room, distrustful, like she was waiting for an ambush.

Her tongue stuck to the roof of her mouth. She'd rehearsed what she would say many times over the last two weeks and now that she sat in front of her she was tongue-tied. The day Zoriana had slapped Mathilda for talking yet again about black magic played on a loop in her head. If she would smack her own kid over talking about the taboo subject, what was she liable to do to her? Was she ready to find out?

Still, no matter how afraid she was right now at the possible response, all she could think about was Zoriana was the only one of them that hadn't verbally told her she was crazy for considering black magic as a way to help them get rid of Killian and Morgana. Which told her that she just might be amenable to it.

Before she lost her nerve, she let the words come spilling and tumbling past her lips. "I know the way you've felt about black magic in the past and with good reason. I'm not here to disrespect Mathilda's memory or the memories of your parents..."

Glancing down at the table, she noticed that Zoriana was gripping the table. Obviously, it was in an effort not to do her physical harm over her statements.

Willow swallowed and forged on. "I just want the best chance at taking down Killian and Morgana. We all know that things are not equal and I just want us to stand a chance against the two of them."

Zoriana stood and the chair she'd been sitting in nearly toppled to the ground. "I can't believe that after the way the others responded, you're still here trying to get me to agree with you." She shook her head in disgust.

"I think you want them dead just as badly as I do, if not more. You're afraid and angry at yourself for considering the use of it." A look crossed Zoriana's face. Willow's eyes grew wide in recognition. She was right about Zoriana. "That's it, isn't it? You don't want the others to know the lengths you're willing to go to avenge your family, which includes using black magic."

This was something they both shared. Killian had plans to take her freedom and possibly her life, he'd more than likely been responsible for her mother's death and Morgana and her family were responsible for Zoriana's family being dead. No one else could understand that pain. No one else could understand what that could make you capable of and the lengths you'd go to make someone pay for the loss you'd suffered, for the people they'd ripped away from you.

Did that make them just as bad as Morgana? Quickly, she crushed that thought, not willing to examine it closely.

Zoriana had angrily given Willow her back and made to storm off when Willow's next words halted her steps. "You'd have the opportunity to kill Morgana. I'll make sure you get to be the one to end her."

Neither of them said a word. Zoriana still hadn't turned around. It seemed like she couldn't breathe until she knew what she planned to do. Was she with her or did she plan to narc on her to Eli?

Slowly, Zoriana turned to face her. "I can't teach it to you..."

Willow's shoulders slumped in defeat. The hopeful look she'd sported seconds ago was immediately wiped away and replaced with a frown. Zoriana had been her last chance to make this happen. She was just about to ask her not to tell Eli she'd asked for her help when Zoriana kept talking.

"There are no black magic books here at the coven. We'll have to find someone that will teach us."

Willow's face lit up like a Christmas tree. She wanted to hug Zoriana, but she wasn't smiling or offering up hugs at being co-conspirators. "No one can know. Do you hear me?" She whispered sternly. "Everything must go on as it has before. If we're caught the consequences are far worse for me than they are for you. Do you understand?"

She nodded, but had a hard time keeping the grin from her face. "When we finally kill Morgana and Killian, everyone is going to be excited. They won't care how it happened."

Zoriana didn't seem to share her sentiment, but she didn't bother to contradict her. "I may know of someone that can help us. I'll let you know soon." Without another word she left the kitchen.

It was hard not to feel a little satisfied after getting Zoriana on her side. She wondered who the witch was that would teach them.

***

The very next night she and Zoriana made up an excuse to leave Walker House. Eli and Phaedra were so fixated on bringing Evie and Delaney up to their standards they didn't question their motives. They didn't take the RV. Once they were outside the house, Zoriana teleported them to the agreed upon location where they were to meet the witch that had agreed to help them.

The park they arrived in was dark and sketchy looking.

"Are you sure she's going to be here?" Willow looked around concerned that they might be attacked or worse.

"Yes. She wanted to meet here first because clearly she doesn't trust us either."

They'd protected themselves by giving her false names. Zoriana was way calmer than she was. On the inside she was freaking out. It had been exhilarating to sneak out and have no one be the wiser to where they were headed and why they were headed there, but now standing in the ominous, darkness in the woods, she felt like she was in a scary movie. Yeah, she was a badass Oracle who was half fae and Zoriana was a witch, but if the supernatural world had taught her anything, it was that there was always something more terrifying to be afraid of.

Before her mind could keep running down that path, a skinny brunette stepped from the shadows. *Did she materialize out of nowhere?* Literally seconds ago no one had been there. She mentally kicked herself. Of course, the woman probably teleported here the same way they had. Her nerves were getting the better of her. She had to stop. The lying and sneaking around were making her crazy.

"Isadora? Betty?" The woman looked between the two of them.

Willow tried not to roll her eyes over the fake names Zoriana had assigned them. Which one of them was supposed to be Isadora? Not that Betty was that much better.

"Yeah." Zoriana said like she met with questionable people undercover of darkness on a regular basis. Maybe she did and Willow just didn't know it.

"I was told you guys were looking to for a book of spells that would help you learn black magic?" She narrowed her eyes at them. Probably trying to figure out if they were legitimate or serious.

"Yes, we're also looking for someone that can train us." Willow chimed in. Zoriana shot her a look, but she didn't care.

"I'll give you the book tonight and then give you an assignment. If you complete it then I'll know you're serious and you can begin your training." She looked at Zoriana a little more closely. "Do we know each other?"

"No." Zoriana snatched the book from her.

"The assignment is tucked inside the book." She didn't seem upset by Zoriana's rudeness before she turned and walked away.

"How do we get in touch with you again?"

"Once you complete the assignment, I'll be alerted." She threw the words over her shoulder and then disappeared into thin air.

"Let's get out of here." Willow looked around once again as an owl hooted and a wolf howled in the distance. She shivered as Zoriana touched her and teleported them back to the street the Walker house was on. They had teleported in and out of the neighborhood behind a copse of trees that were about a half-mile down the street so they wouldn't be noticed by anyone going or coming from the coven, but also so none of the neighbors would see them.

"How are we going to sneak the book inside without someone seeing it and asking questions."

"Simple." Zoriana pulled out a backpack and slipped the book inside. "Here." She handed it over to Willow once she zipped it closed.

"You want me to carry it?" She eyed the bag nervously like it was a ticking time bomb waiting to explode.

"This was your brilliant idea, so yes, you have to carry it. Remember I told you the consequences are far worse for me than they are for you." The reminder had Willow's shaking hand reaching for the bag.

Once they reached the porch, Zoriana pulled out her key and the keyhole appeared in the oak door. Back inside the house, Zoriana led her to a room she hadn't been to before. Thankfully, they encountered no one along the way.

Inside, Zoriana lit some candles with her magic. "Ignis."

Morgana's grinning face flashed in her mind at the use of the word and she was reminded of the night in the woods when she'd used it to light the campfire even though she wasn't supposed to be using magic. She brushed the thought away and walked over to the tall work desk that Zoriana was clearing off. Both of them took off their jackets before Zoriana pulled the large tome from the backpack.

Willow half expected something to happen when the ancient book of evil landed on the table with a soft thud. For a while they both just stared at it. Finally, Zoriana hesitantly reached out, but then dropped her hand back to her side and turned to her. "We still have the opportunity to say no."

Willow nodded and bit her lip. She looked at the book for a long time, before she turned back to Zoriana. "Lets do it."

They both leaned on the desk and Zoriana reached out and opened the book. The dusty pages took on a life of there own and started flipping around before it finally lay opened to a page with a note tucked inside.

Before she could be in awe over the magical book, she had a strong sense of déjà vu, much like the one she'd had in Samson's shop weeks ago. The memory came back sharp and clear of her watching herself and Zoriana in a darkened room, bent over a book right before she'd been yanked into another vision. And here they were now, the pair of them doing exactly what she'd seen that day. Another prophecy fulfilled.

"You okay?" Zoriana's eyes roamed over her face with concern.

"I'm okay. What's the note the say?" It wasn't that she was afraid to tell Zoriana about the vision coming true, but she was afraid the woman would ask questions about her visions and if she'd ever had any concerning Mathilda. It was better she said nothing at all.

The note gave them instructions on the assignment they were to do if they wanted the witch to train them. It was clear from the assignment she wanted to see how far they were willing to go to learn black magic.

"There's still an out, Willow. We don't have to do this."

She wasn't sure if Zoriana was trying to talk her or herself out of this.

"No turning back now."

Zoriana nodded. "We shouldn't do this here. Someone's bound to find out. Remember magic can be tracked. If we create this potion under this roof we'll be discovered right away. We'll gather the ingredients we need and tomorrow after training we'll head deep into the woods and get this done."

"WILLOW? WHERE ARE YOU?"

Who needed a phone when you had telepathy? Most of the time she didn't mind when they communicated this way. It beat needing to be attached to a cell phone. Right now she deemed it a big inconvenience.

"I have to get going. Eli is looking for me." She grabbed her things and headed for the door. "Tomorrow night."

As she headed down the hall she responded to him. "HEY. I'M HEADED BACK NOW. I DIDN'T MEAN TO BE GONE SO LONG." She began to hope she wasn't lost. When they returned she'd followed Zoriana to the room. Nothing looked familiar and she worried she'd have to get Eli to come find her which would raise all sorts of questions she couldn't answer without making up more lies. It was already enough that she was lying to him about doing black magic: she really didn't want to add to it.

After a few more minutes, she breathed a sigh of relief as she came down a corridor she recognized. When she finally arrived at their apartment door, she took a deep breath and composed herself before going inside.

CHAPTER 10

Eli

THEY'D ALL BEEN working so hard, none more so than Willow. During the day she trained, alternating between combat lessons, learning how to be a witch, meditating and honing her Oracle abilities and studied her fae abilities under Cosmo. At night, she often left to go do more studying or sparring. She'd turned into a machine. He was really proud of her dedication, but everyone deserved a night off every now and then.

Today he'd had everyone wrap up earlier. They all cheered when they found out that they wouldn't be required to train all day as usual.

Everyone chattered loudly, making plans for a rare off night. He grabbed Willow's hand. "Hey... I have special plans for us."

Her face lit up in a way he hadn't seen in a long time and it made him glad he'd given everyone the rest of the day off so they could spend time together. Things had slowly started to return to normal between them.

"Tell me what you have planned?"

"Where's the fun in that? It's supposed to be a surprise."

She poked out her lip in a cute pout. "Please tell me." She begged sexily by coming closer and rubbing her nose and lips along the column of his throat.

He bit his lip and chuckled. "Not going to work. It's staying a surprise."

Quickly, she pulled away. "I was so sure that would work. Clearly, I'm off my game."

He chuckled some more and gave her a quick kiss. "We need to shower and get changed. Wear something dressy."

"Ooh."

Her excitement was contagious as they walked to the apartment to get ready for the date night he'd planned. He was tempted to shower with her, but thought better of it. If they did that they'd never leave the bedroom and tonight he wanted to give her a night of romance. They could roll around in the sheets later. Like a true gentlemen, he let her have the bathroom first. After about an hour he started to think maybe he'd made a mistake in letting her go first. When she finally emerged from the bathroom in the pale pink, diaphanous dress she wore that night of the dinner party, any irritation he was feeling disappeared. "Wow. You look amazing... I was hoping you'd wear that tonight." He stood and walked towards her.

When he reached out to grab her she batted him away playfully. "Not until after your shower."

"Before I shower, I have something for you." He walked over to his top drawer and took out a small gift box and handed it to her.

"This is for me?" The bright smile that lit up her face made him happy.

"Open it."

Quickly, she tore off the wrapping paper, letting the bits of paper fall to the ground. When she opened the box it revealed an intricately carved silver bracelet with a greenish colored gemstone in the center.

"It's a talisman."

"Like the one all of you wear?" Her voice was full of awe as she took it out of the box.

"Yes, except I had yours made of silver so that it would match your necklace. It will enhance your power when you do magic." The greenish colored stone was identical to the one that was on the talismans the Protectors wore.

"Thank you. Will you put it on for me?"

He took the bracelet and fastened the clasp around her wrist.

"I love it."

He stole a quick kiss. "I'm going to be fast."

They smiled at one another before he grabbed his things and headed into the bathroom. The date hadn't even started and it already felt like they were back to being them. He couldn't wait to see her eyes light up when she saw the surprise.

Thirty minutes later he stepped out of the bathroom. He was wearing dress pants, which he was sure she would joke him about later. Ever since her near fatal injury, he'd ditched the dressy attire for something more laidback. "I'm almost ready." He called out to her in the living room, as he retrieved his cufflinks from his dresser.

"Eli."

He turned to address her and saw her standing in the doorway with a strange look on her face. "What's wrong?"

"There are some guards here to get you."

His forehead wrinkled in confusion. "What?" He walked out into the living room and to the door and opened it. There on the threshold stood two of the Council guardsmen.

"We have orders to escort you to the Council Chambers."

This had his father written all over it, but he wasn't sure what it was about. "I'll come with you. Give me a moment." He shut the door on them again and turned to find Willow staring at him with worry marring her pretty face. "It's okay. I'm going to go with them and see what they want."

She ran over and hugged him. "Promise me you'll be back."

"I promise." He kissed her forehead and then left with the guards.

Unlike the last time he was escorted by guardsmen, they made sure to make it look like he merely accompanied them. He wasn't sure why the theatrics had been called for. Were they afraid he wouldn't come if they'd requested his presence?

When he entered the room, everyone sat on the dais, but Cora. He figured she'd be absent.

"What's this about? Why not just send a messenger for me or better yet send a note with what you needed to tell me. I had plans you know."

Even though there were thirteen of them that sat in front of him, he knew it would only be his father who spoke. He was the mouthpiece as Interim Chief Elder.

"We called you here because we needed to deliver some news." His father wore a grave expression.

Eli said nothing.

"Your request to be reinstated as the leader of the Protectors has been approved."

He tried to suppress the smile that threatened to break out across his face. As quickly as the thought of gratitude welled up in his chest, it was quickly replaced with a white-hot anger. His jaw tightened. "You brought me here because even though you're reinstating me to leader, you've decided not to give me back my hereditary magic." He made it a statement, and not a question. That was why they sent the guards and decided not to deliver the news in a message. If he was going to get angry and explode they wanted him contained. He gave a mirthless laugh. "May I ask why you've declined to give me back my birthright?"

It was hard not to commit violence. He had been sure they would see reason and return the link to the ancestors.

"It was a tough choice. We were divided, but it ultimately came down to the fact that the punishment needed to stand. We couldn't have others believing that decisions that were passed down by the Council could be reversed.

He nodded and his tongue swiped over his bottom lip. As he looked around the room, he decided the lack of furniture to destroy or objects to throw was on purpose. If any of those things had been present he would have destroyed it all.

"You're making a mistake. We have enemies we must face and you're hell-bent on upholding a ruling. You could get people killed." The words were stated calmly and rationally. Things he was far from feeling on the inside.

Did they purposely have to ruin his night with Willow? He wasn't sure how he could go back now and have their date without his sour mood ruining everything.

His eyes rested on his father once more before he turned and left. He went in search of Phaedra. If it wasn't so important he wouldn't have banged on her door, knowing that she was trying to enjoy some quiet time with Max, just like he'd wanted to enjoy the special evening he'd planned with Willow.

When she answered the door, her face sported a scowl, until she saw the look on his face. She stepped aside so he could enter. Thankfully, this time she was fully clothed and Max was seated on the sofa with a beer in his hands.

There was no point in beating around the bush. "They gave me the leadership position back, but the stripping will stand."

"Why did they not call me to be a part of the meeting?" She crossed her arms over her chest.

"My guess is they didn't want an audience or someone that could back me up, speak up on the stupid decision they made." He looked at her and sighed. "They were so sure I was going to get angry and go all Hulk smash. They even had guards come get me from my apartment."

"Silas has done a lot of questionable things, but this..." She paced the floor in thought.

"No one said anything for several minutes.

"There isn't anymore that we can do right now. I just wanted to tell you before you heard it from someone else... and thanks."

The confusion on her face made him smile.

"Thanks for having my back. I came here to vent and commiserate with someone and every time you have my back. If you wanted to maintain the leader position I'm okay with that. I couldn't think of another person more skilled and capable than you to lead the Protectors."

"You must really be feeling some kind of way to get all sappy on me. Get out of here... and no, I do not want the position. It's yours." Phaedra was trying to act all tough and unaffected by his words, but he could see the smile she was trying to wrestle into submission. He definitely wasn't going to push it by pointing it out.

"Later Max." Max held up his beer bottle in a goodbye gesture.

When he stepped back out into the hallway and shut the door he knew he should head back to his apartment, but he just needed more time. Even though he'd told himself not to get his hopes up about getting his hereditary magic back, a small part of him had. He'd been so sure that The Elders would see reason, but they hadn't. There was no use in feeling sorry for himself. He just needed to get his head right.

CHAPTER 11

Willow

WHEN SHE OPENED the door and found the Walker guards standing there she nearly fainted. She'd been certain they had found out about her and Zoriana's extracurricular activities with black magic and were there to arrest her, but the man had asked for Eli.

Her relief was short-lived. What did The Council want with Eli?

When he'd left with them, she had been unsure she would see him tonight. The worry ate at her. She felt bad that the plans he'd made were ruined. Throughout the night she found herself eyeing or playing with the bracelet he'd just given her and she would smile and sad smile and hope it wasn't the last gift she'd ever get from him.

Two hours had passed and still he hadn't returned. She tucked her bare feet beneath her. An hour ago, she'd abandoned her heels. She flipped through the channels. It had been so long since she watched TV. Not that she'd been a TV junkie before this all happened, but she had watched the occasional show. Part of her wondered if the supernatural world had a channel for programming. Did they have shows similar to the bachelor, but it was about marrying a shifter? The thought made her giggle.

As she turned to another channel, Eli walked back in. She jumped up from the sofa, TV forgotten and looked him over from head to toe. He was okay. "You're okay?" She waited for a verbal confirmation.

"Yeah, I'm fine." His tone was a little sullen.

"Why did they want to see you?" Part of her was still a little worried that maybe it was about her, but instead of dragging her out of here they'd questioned him first to see what he knew.

He dropped onto the sofa and she sat beside him. For several seconds he said nothing, only took her hand in his and stroked his thumb across the back of her hand. The suspense was killing her, but she waited for him to speak first.

"They reinstated me as leader of the Protectors."

"That's great news." She gave him a bright smile. "This is what you wanted. I just don't understand why they needed the guards to come down here and get you and make you go to their chambers to get the news." It was puzzling and she knew there had to be more to the story. "That's really good news, but you don't seem happy about it... what else did they want?" She tried to keep her hands still in her lap.

Finally, he looked at her. "They won't reverse the decision and give me back my hereditary magic."

Her hand flew up to cover her mouth. The surprise on her face remained evident. Even though they hadn't discussed it she knew how much he'd been counting on the Elders to do the right thing, the logical thing. She touched his arm, wanting to console him. "I'm sorry." Tentatively, she reached out and when he didn't resist she pulled him into a hug.

As she held him she thought about her decision to defy him and learn black magic. The decision the Elders made only reconfirmed that she'd been right to make it. If she waited like Eli for permission, nothing was going to change and she or any of them could end up dead. At this point, it was better to beg for forgiveness later than get permission.

They never made it to the surprise he'd set up, but she figured it would be better on another night.

***

The next day she was restless in her training with Cosmo. She hadn't been able to quite put her finger on it until he called her out for not concentrating. "Your head hasn't been here all day. What's going on? This isn't like you." His patience with her had been limitless and for that she was grateful. She knew she could be a handful, but he was right. She wasn't concentrating and she realized it was because she needed something more challenging.

"I love that you have taken the time and interest in helping me develop and hone my faery abilities..."

"But..." He gave her a questioning look and waited for her to elaborate.

"I want you to push me. I want to be challenged..." Her eyes darted around the room to see if anyone was listening to their conversation and then she dropped her voice. "I want you to teach me possession or astral projection."

If Cosmo felt some kind of way about what she said, the emotion didn't register on his face. The guy had an incredible poker face.

Since he still hadn't said anything, she launched into her pitch, talking at a rapid fire pace. "We could be training for the next few months or Killian and Morgana could bring the fight to us, show up on our doorstep and I need to know the big moves, the powers and skills that could mean the difference between life and death. Not just merely how to defend myself. When we go up against them they aren't planning to take prisoners, it will be kill or be killed." She took a deep breath and continued to stare at him.

It seemed like forever before he spoke. "Are you finished with your monologue? How long have you been practicing that anyway?" A grin poked out from underneath the blank mask he'd been wearing the whole time she spoke.

"A while."

They both laughed.

"Let's do it."

Her eyes grew big in shock and surprise. "Just like that?"

"Just like that."

"You mean to tell me this whole time, all I had to do was ask?" It seemed too simple.

"All you had to do was ask." Cosmo looked at her innocently.

"Why didn't you tell me that?

"You didn't ask." He chuckled and smirked at her.

She was too excited to be annoyed. "Okay, how do we do this? Who am I going to practice on?"

"On me, of course." He grew serious as he sat down in front of her. "Now, I really need you to listen to me. This is very important. Possession is nothing to be taken lightly. Leaving your body isn't the hardest part about this, returning to it is." He stared at her and she nodded in understanding. "Once your spirit leaves your body you're going to feel a bit like an untethered balloon. You'll feel like you want to float away. Fight that feeling." Cosmo glanced around. "This isn't the right place to do this. Let me go check with Eli and see if we can move to a quieter space."

Willow gripped his arm before he could get up. "Don't tell Eli what it's for." Her eyes pleaded with him.

The question was on Cosmo's lips to ask, 'Why not?' but he didn't. "Okay."

She bit her nails as she watched him head over and ask Eli about them moving to a private area. He looked over in her direction and she dropped her hand in her lap. She wasn't sure what explanation Cosmo offered him, but when he came back over, he gave her the thumbs up. They gathered up their things and walked about two doors down. The room was smaller and most of the floor was covered in gym mats. They dropped their stuff in a corner and he chose a spot for them to sit.

"We're going to start off much like you do when you're meditating and trying to force a vision. Lay down."

She looked at him apprehensively, but then moved to lie down. Out of the corner of her eye, she noticed he did the same thing.

"Relax. Deep breath..." He exhaled slowly. "Now close your eyes." She did as he said. "Clear your mind and as you clear your mind I want you to think about being dead."

Instantly, Willow sat bolt upright. "What?"

Cosmo sat up calmly and turned to her. "How did you think this would work? In order to possess someone else your natural body has to believe it's dead or your soul won't leave it."

An uncontrollable shiver ran up her spine. He grabbed her hands and squeezed. "It will be a little scary the first time, but if you master this, it can be a very powerful weapon in your arsenal." Her head bobbed up and down at his words and she swallowed. "Once your spirit is outside your body you'll be able to still hear my voice, but you won't be able to communicate with anything living until you're in another host body or back in your own. You will be able to communicate with the dead if they're nearby."

Her head snapped up to look at him when he mentioned that last part. "I'll be able to talk to the dead?" He must have noticed the hopefulness on her face because he grew very serious.

"Listen to me Willow, as tempting as it sounds to go looking for the ones we've lost, the longer your body is outside of your own or a host body the easier it is to never find your way back which means..."

"Which means you die." She finished for him. He nodded. "Once you're out get to the person you're trying to possess and when you're finished return to your body as soon as you can. Don't linger."

She lay back on the mat again.

"When your spirit pushes into my body it's going to feel weird and strange at first because it's foreign to you, but keep going until you're securely lodged.

"How will I know that?" She turned to look at him.

"I won't be resisting you anymore." She grimaced at his words and he continued in a reassuring tone. "Possession isn't easy. Even though we're training and I'm giving you permission I will try and resist or keep you from coming in. You'll only feel it for a minute, but I'll make it as easy for you as I can. Just know that typically you'll have to fight your way in. At least all of your other training is helping and you have quite a strong-willed nature so..." He smiled.

"While you're inside of someone else you may hear that person's voice, but it depends on how strong they are. Be prepared for that. Once you're finished and ready to leave and return to your own body, dislodge, focus on your body. You'll feel like there is a cord pulling you in the direction of your body, almost like an astronaut tethered by a lifeline to a spaceship when they step out to explore space. Follow it. Let it lead you back."

Something niggled at the back of her mind. "What if something gets in the way of that cord or it gets severed." She gulped, fearful of his answer.

The look he gave her was grave. "Let's just say it won't be easy." She swallowed again. "Ready?"

She nodded and stared at the ceiling.

"Close your eyes, deep breath, clear your mind." She could tell he'd return to lying on the mat. "Slow down your heart rate. This takes a bit of practice. Focus on the beats and count in your head until the rhythm starts to match." For a while he said nothing and she practiced doing what he said. It was difficult and she was close to quitting after fifteen minutes, but when she thought about what was at stake she willed herself to focus and slow her heart rate. Another fifteen minutes passed and she could feel it slowing down. She wasn't sure how he knew it was working, but he started speaking again. "Think about death and let your consciousness drift away."

As scary as it sounded, she listened to his instructions and suddenly she felt outside of herself. She hadn't opened her eyes, but the next thing she knew she was watching herself. She appeared to be in a deep sleep, like some fairytale princess waiting to be kissed by a prince. When she looked over, she saw Cosmo lying next to her with his eyes closed and she went towards him.

"You should be able to hear my voice. Don't be scared."

She could hear him, but it was slightly muffled, like listening to someone from underneath the water.

How to do this exactly? When she reached out her hand and pushed into him, immediately she was forced back out.

"I felt you. Be more forceful."

Taking a moment, she gathered all of her energy and dove into Cosmo's body. This time there was little resistance and she felt her spirit began to settle as much as it could inside a body that didn't belong to her. Slowly, she could feel herself gaining control of his body. In a jerky movement, she lifted his arm. She could feel his mouth spread into a grin. It was because of her. This was working and she was smiling. She sat up and looked over at her own body. With her finger she poked her side. *Wild!*

"Having fun?"

She almost jumped out of his body at hearing Cosmo's voice in her head... their head? "Yeah."

"Okay. I think that's enough for today. Let me have my body back." He joked.

She lay back and reached upward. It was like her soul was peeling itself away from him. In a matter of seconds she was free and looking back at her own body again. Cosmo sat up.

"Get back in your body, Willow."

The curiosity to explore almost got the better of her, but she remembered what he'd said earlier and she let the imaginary tether pull her back towards her body until her spirit was inside. She blinked her eyes open and lay there for a while staring at the ceiling.

"Welcome back."

She turned and looked at Cosmo.

"How do you feel?"

She thought about it for a minute. "A little strange, but fine."

"That feeling will wear off shortly. Just remember. It's not always going to be that easy. If someone doesn't want you inside you'll have to fight tooth and nail to get in. If you're dealing with another supernatural, they can try and harm you in your spirit state so be careful. It helps if you try to take possession either when they're unconscious or asleep. Okay, that's it for the day." He helped her up from the mat and they collected their things. She wondered when she might be able to practice again. When the entered the training room where everyone else was, she wondered if she would tell Eli what they were doing if he asked. He smiled at her when they entered and she smiled back, unsure whether she would give him the truth or another lie.

CHAPTER 12

Eli

HE NEVER ASKED her what she and Cosmo did in private. What skill or power did she practice that she didn't want him to see? He'd hoped she would tell him willingly because she wanted to share it with him. It was hard, because he remembered a time when she would squeal in delight at getting something right and want to share it with him right away. Now, it was Cosmo, Zoriana, Max or even Evie that she shared those things with. He was present for the many achievements and accomplishments; it was just different.

Today, he had them going through a drill that would measure their success with using what they were learning in an actual battle. Using magic, he and Phaedra had rigged another room to run them through a simulation that could be a scenario they could face. Delaney and Evie definitely needed the practice that this offered, but so did Willow. She'd seen combat a handful of times with the Protectors, but he wanted to see how well she was learning the spells or even her faery abilities. Could she use everything on the fly or in the heat of battle?

Delaney was the first one into the simulation. He and Phaedra had a front row seat to the entertainment via a one way mirrored window that let them see into the room and use their magic to manipulate.

The eager, young recruit seemed to be doing well, but most of his moves became predictable. It was easy to corner him or lead him where they wanted him and inevitably kill him. They needed to work on him thinking more outside the box. After a few more run-throughs they compiled their notes and concluded his test.

Next, they brought in Evie. She looked like a warrior as she entered the room and seemed a more sure of herself than Delaney had been. When she ran through the simulation she surprised them a bit with the choices she made. Phaedra seemed pleased with her performance, which was not an easy thing to accomplish. Usually, Phaedra always had criticisms, but this time she floundered a bit with what to say. "Let's run her through it again. Maybe she got lucky on the first one." He hid his smirk as they ran her through a few more times. Each time, Phaedra tried to throw in different things to trip her up, but unlike Delaney, Evie didn't fall for them.

"Just say it. We can't find any fault with her performance. You should be pleased. It means that we made a good decision."

This time she gave him the finger when he smiled at her.

Once he saw Willow enter the room, he grew serious. He wanted her to do well. The room transformed the same way it had for Delaney and Evie. It now resembled a throne room. They'd had Willow share what she remembered of the interior of Killian's castle to build the simulation. If she was triggered by anything, this would help them know where her weak points might lie.

Internally, he was cheering her on. He wanted her to do well.

"YOU GOT THIS." He couldn't help reaching out to tell her that he had faith in her.

A small smile crossed her face. "THANK YOU."

First, they sent a pack of vampires after her. She blasted one of them with energy from one hand, while pulling a wooden stake from her belt and stabbing one of them in the chest. That one instantly turned to ash. The other three kept coming for her. Using some hand-to hand combat training she performed a high kick and sent one flying backwards. One of them was almost upon her when she pointed her finger at him and chanted, "Collum frangeretur." The vampire fell to the ground unconscious.

She was doing so well it was hard not to feel a swell of pride. Phaedra glanced his way and he masked his smile, by staring out the window with a blank expression.

The final vampire reached her before she got her hand on her dagger. He held her by the throat. She kicked her legs a few times, which was an expected reaction to being choked out.

"Come on, Willow." He mumbled to himself.

After a couple more seconds of kicking, she calmed and stopped struggling. While one hand gripped still tried to keep his hand from crushing her throat, she used her strength to grab her dagger and plunge it into his eye. The vampire yelled and tried to grab the knife from his eye. He released his hold on her and instead of dropping to a heap on the ground; her legs hit the ground in a crouched stance. She coughed a couple times, but sprung up into a sidekick, which struck the vampire in the chest. When he stumbled backwards, she blasted him with the energy from her hands.

All of the vampires lay on the ground, unconscious.

Suddenly, a Killian like figure appeared before her. Eli gave Phaedra an angry look. "What are you doing? We hadn't made that part of the simulation."

"We need to know how she'll react when she has to face him."

Eli turned back to stare out the glass and watch Willow come face to face with her monster. Was this how it was in her dreams? He knew that it probably didn't look exactly like the Killian she saw in her dream since she was the only one that knew what he looked like. They had no picture to go off of when they designed him for the simulation and had to use what she'd told them about him. It's just that, he and Phaedra had never agreed on whether they would use him during the training or not.

Phaedra's logic made sense, but he was upset that he did it without talking to him.

For a moment, he saw the raw fear in Willow's eyes and he almost put a stop to it. The others hadn't come up against him in their simulation. It didn't seem fair or right.

"We should stop this." If this were anyone else, he would not let his emotions get in the way of the mission. The minute he put duty on the sideline to be with her, he'd allowed himself to be ruled by his heart.

Phaedra turned to him without anger and explained the rationale to why they would not put a stop to this. "But we won't because you and I both know that she is who Killian wants and if she can't face him and use everything she's learning to save herself, there might not be anything the rest of us can do for her."

The worry ate at him as he watched her.

"I know this is difficult, but we don't know how things will play out when we face off against them, but we have to be prepared for every possible scenario, including the fact that she may have to face him alone."

Phaedra was right, although he hated to admit it. He had to let this play out. When he resumed watching, it wasn't long before Killian grabbed her and spun her around in a maneuver that utilized his vampire speed. All he could do was watch in horror as Killian attempted to overpower her. Willow fought him with everything she had and he held out hope that it would be enough, that she would come out victorious.

CHAPTER 13

Willow

AFTER THE FAILED simulation involving Killian, she'd beat herself up daily. She'd run through the simulation three times that day and each time he bested her. One of the times, he'd got the opportunity to turn her. If she couldn't save herself, how was she going to save anyone else?

Her thoughts wondered to something else, less painful to think about. Brielle, the warlock that trained her and Zoriana in black magic had been particularly tough lately. She often wondered about her. They didn't know her background. They continued to use their fake names with her. It was probably best for everyone. Between the witch training she was getting at Walker House and the black magic training she was becoming pretty proficient, but she knew it was more of a textbook knowledge. She hoped that

Eli would let them do some mock battles so she could try and cast a spell under duress.

Right now, she was hoping to induce a vision and see the future, possibly the location of where Killian was hiding.

Alone in the training room, she sat on the mat cross-legged and placed her hands, palms up on her knees. Immediately, she began to clear her mind of everything, just as Eli had taught her. Everything emptied out of her brain: past, present, future. As she took a deep, cleansing breath she was aware how much easier that had become, compared to the first time when she struggled with the idea of meditation. Her mind was now a blank slate. The minute it became white space, that inner voice spoke, '*Show me.*'

Suddenly she was standing inside her vision. Someone was running at her with a battleaxe. Quickly, she ducked and then remembered that she wasn't actually here, as the person passed right through her. *Where am I?*

When she looked around she saw Phaedra battling Katana. Max was in his wolf form, taking on a group of vampires and Zoriana had just taken down a bloodsucker with a fireball. Evie and Delaney were there too. That's when the surroundings became clearer. They were in Killian's castle. She recognized the sconces on the wall in the hallway. She whipped her head around, searching this way and that. Where was Eli? The minute the thought popped into her head she found Eli in the melee fighting with two vampires. Where was Killian? Where was she?

At least she now knew that they took the fight to Killian, but where is the castle. She still had seen nothing that told her where they were. Maybe if she left the room she would find something that would tell her. Dead or unconscious bodies littered the floor and she had to step around them as she tried to exit the room. When she reached the door, Morgana stepped in her path. Again, she forgot that she wasn't actually there. Morgana looked right through her and began to chant some kind of spell. *Damn!* It sucked that her visions still had no sound. Would she ever be able to hear in these? It would have really been helpful to know what she was saying.

When she looked back over her shoulder to see who was affected by the spell, what she saw made her blood run cold. She turned around completely an watched helplessly as all of the Protectors became immobile. Whatever spell Morgana had them under, was keeping them from moving. She turned back to Morgana and screamed at the top of her lungs, even though she knew there was no stopping what was to come. Morgana uttered a final word and when Willow looked around, each of the Protectors' faces took on a blank look and they crumpled to the ground. She continued to scream. It was the only thing she could do. They were all dead. Morgana had just killed them all. She ran towards Eli's fallen body, tears streaming down her face. The minute she fell to her knees and went to pick him up, she was pulled from the vision.

When her eyes took in the training room, she howled in pain. She wailed and sobbed loudly. Then she was choking and gasping for air. She tried to fill her lungs with oxygen. She gulped for air. Her body was in a state of panic and shock. They died, they all died. Morgana killed them. They were all going to die. After she got her breathing under control, she rocked back and forth on her knees as she hugged her body. *That can't be what happens. It was just a nightmare.*

As much as she tried to make herself believe that, she knew what she saw was real. It was the reality she was faced with. She was going to lose everyone she cared about. There had to be a way for her to keep it from happening.

Neither Killian nor her had been in the room so maybe she was still alive at that point. Maybe Brielle knew of some spell that she could use against Morgana? She would have to get the woman alone to ask the question. There was no way she would tell any of them the fate that awaited them. There had to be a way to reverse it or keep it from coming true. There just had to be.

Once she was able to stop crying she tried to clean herself up. She wasn't sure how she would explain her red, swollen, puffy eyes to Eli. He would take one look at her and be concerned. She needed to come up with an excuse.

Thankfully, she and Zoriana had a session with Brielle. She'd avoid going home and just tell Eli she got caught up with something. She'd ask Zoriana to get rid of her red-rimmed eyes by telling her she got something in it from mixing a potion. No one had to know the truth. While they were there she'd make sure Brielle shared some spells for killing vampires... and high-powered warlocks. Morgana was definitely someone she needed to figure out how to kill.

Her concern grew over the lack of visuals of her or Killian during the vision. Where were the two of them? Were they fighting in a separate area of the castle? Had he turned her already? So many questions plagued her.

She headed to the kitchens to wait until Zoriana would show up so they could leave the house together. Unfortunately, the idea of seeing Brielle without Zoriana wasn't really going to work. She had no key to get back into Walker House. They were only given to the witches and worked solely for them since each key was designed with the wood from the door and the key holder's DNA. Even if she were able to steal a key it wouldn't work for her.

As she sat at the table, the thoughts of defeat kept replaying themselves over and over. So, not only could she not kill Killian before he sunk his fangs into her and turned her, but she couldn't save any of them either. The feelings of inadequacy and helplessness engulfed her. For a second she felt like she was drowning. And, if she kept thinking about this right now, she would break down even more. With an iron will that she'd honed through hours of meditation, she compartmentalized those feelings and pushed them away to deal with how to get Brielle to help her.

Suddenly, an idea struck her that could work. She'd speak to Brielle telepathically. Zoriana would never know they were communicating. Yeah, that way she could get the answers she needed and Zoriana would be none the wiser. She was so grateful to arrive at a solution for her immediate problem, even if it didn't solve the larger one.

Unfortunately, she had hours to kill while she waited for Zoriana to show and the vision came back and kept running on a loop inside her head. A few times she had to brush tears away. That couldn't become the fate of her friends. That couldn't be what happened to Eli, they hadn't had a chance to just be a normal couple yet.

"You okay?"

When she looked up Zoriana wore a worried expression. "Have you been crying?" Zoriana sat down next to her.

"No, it's not what it looks like." The laugh that left her mouth was false, but it was necessary. "I'm almost too embarrassed to tell you." The look of concern hadn't left Zoriana's eyes. "I was practicing mixing some potions alone earlier and one kind of blew up in my face, caused by eyes to tear up pretty badly." She waved her hand over her eyes.

"Oh, you have to be careful. You still shouldn't be practicing without supervision. It's too early. Does it hurt?"

"That's what I get for wanting to impress you guys. You know, trying to be the star student and all... it burns a little." The lies just slipped out so naturally these days, but right now she didn't care. There was no way she was going to tell Zoriana, that her and the whole team ended up dead if they fought Killian.

"Hold still. I'll heal it for you." She placed her hand over Willow's eyes. "Sana." The white light obstructed Willow's vision for a second as the spell healed her swollen, puffy eyes. When it stopped and she could see again, Zoriana was smiling at her. "Good as new. Now let's get going. We don't want to be late or Brielle will be pissed."

Once they were at Brielle's, Willow waited for a moment when Zoriana was preoccupied so that in case she startled Brielle, Zoriana wouldn't notice.

"I NEED TO SPEAK WITH YOU. THIS IS BETTY, BY THE WAY. I'M THE ONE INSIDE YOUR HEAD."

To Brielle's credit, she didn't look wildly around or even so much as flinch at hearing her voice inside her head.

"WHY ARE WE COMMUNICATING THIS WAY? WHAT IS IT YOU DON'T WANT YOUR FRIEND TO KNOW?" Brielle continued to work and do the things she'd been doing so attention wouldn't be drawn to them. Willow followed her lead.

"I NEED YOU TO TEACH ME SPELLS TO KILL VAMPIRES... AND A HIGH-POWERED WARLOCK."

An amused look crossed Brielle's face. "AND JUST WHO IS THIS HIGH-POWERED WARLOCK YOU WANT TO KILL?"

"IT'S NOT YOU." If Brielle thought she was going to easily give up a name, she was mistaken. Either the woman could teach her or she couldn't, but there was a reason they'd given her fake names to begin with.

"OKAY, BETTY." Brielle emphasized the name when she said it. Letting her know she was aware the name wasn't her real one. "WHAT'S TO KEEP ME FROM TELLING, ISADORA HERE, WHAT IT IS THAT YOU WANT?"

The threat didn't have the desired hope that Brielle wanted. Willow called her bluff. "TELL HER." Willow gave her a hard stare down over Zoriana's back. "GO AHEAD... I DON'T THINK YOU WILL THOUGH." If it had just been the two of them Willow probably would have crossed her arms over her chest to make the glare a little more effective.

Neither of them said anything for several charged seconds.

"IF YOU COME BACK TOMORROW NIGHT I CAN TEACH YOU." Brielle offered with a smile.

Willow wasn't dumb enough to believe that Brielle had been teaching them black magic out of the goodness of her heart, two complete strangers. There was no way she would come here alone, without Zoriana. "I CAN'T. THERE MUST BE ANOTHER WAY." Beside that reason, there was still the whole no key situation. She would have no way back into Walker House without Zoriana.

"THERE IS A BOOK I CAN GIVE YOU BEFORE YOU GO. I WILL MARK THE PASSAGES. WHICH MEANS YOU'LL HAVE TO LEARN THEM ON YOUR OWN. IT TAKES POWERFUL MAGIC TO PERFORM THESE. ARE YOU SURE YOU'RE UP TO IT? YOU'RE MERELY A STUDENT, NOT A REAL WITCH." Brielle sneered at her when she delivered the last words.

There's her true nature. Willow wondered when it would come out. "YOU DON'T NEED TO WORRY ABOUT THAT."

Zoriana had just finished setting up the cauldron and the various ingredients that they needed for tonight. "So, what are we learning tonight?"

The rest of the night passed without incident. The two of them worked together, following Brielle's instruction to make the potion and she Brielle didn't speak anymore that night beyond her asking questions about the potion they were making. At the end of the night, before they left, Brielle managed to slip the book into her backpack without Zoriana noticing. She nodded her head in thanks and they left. Now she just needed to figure out where she would hide the book when they got back. Plus, figure out when she would find the time to study the passages between all of her other training and sneaking around.

CHAPTER 14

Eli

WHY WAS THE bed shaking? He blinked his eyes several times, trying to wake himself up. As he rolled over, he was struck by one of Willow's flailing limbs. *What?* His grogginess was quickly fading away. He sat up quickly. She must have been dreaming about Killian. No, this seemed different. Yes, she kicked and screamed, but her nose wasn't bleeding and the screaming wasn't because she was writhing in agony. "Willow. Wake up." He firmly shook her and within seconds she woke up.

She panted and looked wildly around the room like she was afraid she'd wake up somewhere else.

"The dream wasn't about Killian was it?"

For a while she just stared up at him, until she finally shook her head no.

"Do you want to talk about it?"

This time she shook her head right away, but then she burst into tears.

Alarm bells went off in his head. "Willow. What's wrong? Please tell me."

She turned towards him and put her arms around his neck. The way she latched onto him made him wonder what exactly happened in the dream. "It's okay. Whatever it is, you're safe." He wrapped his arms around her and held her while she sobbed. If only she would tell him what was wrong.

Lately, she'd been like a machine. She still compartmentalized the day between combat and weapons training, faery training with Cosmo and witch training. At night she meditated and practiced her Oracle abilities and even did further training. Sometimes they were just barely seeing each other in passing. There were nights when he went to bed without her, not because he wanted to, but he was training as well and it was hard to stay awake and wait up for her when he was physical and mentally drained as well.

Eventually, she cried herself to sleep, but she still clung to him. He rubbed her back as she slept, hoping to soothe her and keep whatever was terrorizing her at bay. He could help her if she told him.

***

In the morning when he woke up she was gone. He must have been exhausted if he hadn't heard her get up and shower. It had taken time for him to fall back to sleep after her nightmare. He got up and showered and dressed. When he entered the training room, she was already in the corner working with Cosmo, so much for trying to talk to her. He was sure that was by design. She was going to do this whole avoidance thing so he couldn't ask her about it.

"You look tired." Phaedra needed to work on her greetings.

"Good morning to you too." There wasn't a playful tone to his voice.

"I mean it. You look tired." Phaedra stepped into his line of sight, blocking Willow from him. "What's going on?"

"Oh, you mean besides us training 24/7 for a war that we could lose or possibly get ourselves killed?" He hissed.

"Okay, smartass. I know something's up. You know better than to get sarcastic with me, so the fact that you are tells me something is up. Talk." She folded her arms across her chest. He was sure she was prepared to wait him out.

He sighed. "I'm worried about Willow. What if this is all starting to get to her? I know she's been anxious about what could happen when we finally face Killian, but she seems to be running on auto-pilot lately..." He hesitated to tell Phaedra the next part. "Then there are the constant nightmares she's been having."

Phaedra looked at him with concern. "About Killian?" She came and stood next to him. Her eyes wandered to Willow.

"No, she won't tell me."

"Do you think it has to do with her failed simulation?"

He looked up again and watched Cosmo instruct her. "I don't know. Probably. I just wish she'd talk to me." He leaned his head back against the wall. "Maybe we're over training. Maybe we're just all going stir crazy. We haven't left this place in the last two months."

"You know that's been for her protection as well as everyone else's. We don't know what Killian and Morgana are plotting. You know right now, this is the safest place... but, I do agree with you." She rolled her eyes and held up her finger to silence him before he could respond. "If you tell anyone that I will kill you."

He chuckled. It felt good to laugh, if only for a brief moment.

"I think we should cut training for the day. You never got to have your special date with Willow. Maybe you should do that tonight."

He smiled at her. "I think that's a good idea."

Eli whistled and clapped his hands together. "Okay. Let me get everyone's attention." They all stopped what they were doing and looked towards him. "No more training for today. In fact, we're not going to train tomorrow either." Some cheers went up at his declaration.

He smiled and walked towards Willow. "I believe I owe you a date."

The genuine smile that he received from her warmed his heart. When he got closer, he could see the circles under her eyes. She hadn't slept that well either.

They left the training room holding hands. Back in the apartment, they showered together and managed to keep their hands off each other. Once they were dressed he took her hand once again and led her from the apartment down the corridor. He took a few turns here and there until he came to another door that on the outside looked just like every other door lining the hallway.

When he turned to face her and took both of her hands in his she had an expectant, eager look on her face. He was glad that the smudges under her eyes were pretty much gone at this moment as she nearly jumped up and down with excitement. If he was honest, he was just as excited as she was. "For you, the first time we met was in the break room at work."

"Yeah, and you weren't so nice to me." She giggled.

"True, but as you now know I had a very good reason." He grinned back at her, exposing his teeth. "The first time I saw you was well before that. At the beginning my mission was to stay in the shadows, guard you, keep you safe." He grew serious. "The more I watched you the more I fell in love with you. That first night I saw you, I actually heard you first. I walked in that bar and I heard this voice that was like velvet, that was like making love on a Sunday morning... that felt like home... then I looked up and there you were."

Her mouth dropped open in shock. "Why didn't you ever tell me? I thought you just were the one sent to clean up, to make sure the record producers never approached. Everyone thought you'd never heard me sing?" Her face registered, shock, surprise and happiness all at once.

"I know. I wasn't supposed to be there. Now you understand why it was so hard for me. Depriving the world of a voice like yours felt like killing Bambi or something."

They both laughed and leaned their foreheads against one another. For a minute they just rested against each other like that, breathing in one another. He was the first to pull away. Standing up straighter, he looked at her. "I wanted to recreate that night. If you'd been just a woman and I'd been just a man... when you'd finished singing I would have asked you for a drink." At that he opened the door, never taking his eyes off her face. Part of the fun was watching her mouth drop to the ground in amazement.

"This is..." She pointed out to the street that lay beyond the door, words failing her at that moment. "How?"

"Magic."

They both stared out the door and watched Broadway Street in Nashville come to life. He took her hand and they stepped out onto the sidewalk and the door shut behind them. She looked at the shut door and then at him. "Is this oaky?"

"Yes." In her eyes, he saw the reflection of the brightly colored neon lights. Her joy shone through so bright, he knew he'd made the right choice. This street was a big part of the nightlife in Nashville. For an hour, the walked the streets, grabbing drinks and quick bites to eat here and there, so Willow could have some of the things she'd missed. He knew she loved the city and even though she didn't talk about it, he knew she'd missed it. It felt good to give this back to her, even if it was just for a few hours.

"I have somewhere else special I want to take you." He pulled her into an alley and then teleported them to a secluded spot.

"Where are we?" She looked this way and that, trying to figure out where he'd brought her. When he got them out to the street he saw she was shocked again when she realized they were outside The Bluebird Café.

"I figured you might want to sing in front of an audience."

Her smile faltered. "What about cameras or social media? You're not worried someone will see me and it will get back to Killian or Morgana."

"I've got it covered. We'll be here an hour tops and then we'll head home." They walked towards the line of people standing outside, waiting to get in.

"We're never going to get inside, look at the line. I can forget singing tonight too because usually there's a waiting list. It was such a nice thought. I'm sorry it's not going to work out." She took his hand ready to walk away.

"Mr. Walker. Mr. Walker. We've been waiting on you." An older woman with graying hair, wearing a plaid shirt, jeans and cowboy boots came over to greet them. "We've been waiting for you. I have your table reserved. Right this way." She guided them past the line and into the building.

Once they were seated, she smacked his arm. "Why didn't you tell me? You let me go on and on out there and you knew the whole time you'd already set this up."

"I told you I had it covered." He gave her a smirk. Willow leaned over, hugged him and planted a big kiss of gratitude on his cheek.

A voice interrupted them. "Miss Stevens. We're ready for you to do a sound check before you perform."

She looked at him excitedly. "Go ahead."

One more quick kiss, and she was up and out of her seat in a split second. She followed the man backstage. Fifteen minutes later, she stood on stage. The room was packed, standing room only. He'd already cast a spell so that no one could record or take pictures or post about her or the performance.

Approaching the microphone, he could sense her nervous, excited energy before she addressed the crowd.

"I'm so honored to be here tonight. The song I'm going to sing is dedicated to a man who's very special to me. This isn't a country song, but I want to sing it for him and put my own little twist on it. At that moment she looked directly at him before she began to sing The Police's 'Every Little Thing She Does Is Magic.' One of the twists she put on the song was to change, 'she' to 'he' and it became 'Every Little Thing He Does Is Magic.' She'd sung this rendition that night out in the woods around the campfire.

You could hear a pin drop in the bar as she sung a slower tempo version of the song. When she finished the room erupted into cheers and wild applause. She bounded off the stage and threw herself into his arms. "I love you." She whispered into his ear.

"I love you too."

"Now, take me home. I'm ready to be alone with you." She pulled back and beamed at him.

He didn't have to be told twice. Once they got back to Walker House, they wasted no time in getting back to the apartment. He made achingly slow love to her for the rest of the night. During the last time he wiped tears from her eyes, right before they fell asleep.

CHAPTER 15

Willow

SHE'D PRETENDED TO be asleep so that he would sleep. Before they'd left tonight, she'd seen the worry in his eyes. The date he'd taken her on was magical and for a short while it masked all of the dread she'd been carrying around. Her body still ached to be joined to his after the way they'd made love. It also told her that she didn't want to lose this and she would do anything within her power to hold onto Eli, hold onto them.

Cautiously, she crept from the bed and grabbed sweats that had been tossed on the chair earlier. She dressed in the living room and then quietly left the apartment and headed to the training room, which she knew would be deserted at this hour. When she induced a vision this time she planned to get a location. She didn't care how many times she had to put herself under, she would get that piece of information so she could end this once and for all.

Just like she'd done a few days ago, she sat cross-legged on the mat and placed her hands, palms up on her knees. She cleared her mind of everything, emptied out her brain of anything, past, present, future. When she took a deep, cleansing breath her mind became a blank white space. *'Show me.'*

Immediately she was plunged into a vision she'd had before. She was in the woods somewhere outside of what she was sure was Killian's castle and the sky was a vivid, reddish hue. She looked up and saw a solar eclipse. Since the last time she'd had this vision she'd learned that solar eclipses such as this one could be a sign of something ominous or an omen of bad things to come.

Last time she'd been unable to see more than this part of the vision before she was ripped from it and thrust into another one. She ran through the woods hoping to come upon a road or something that might reveal where she was. Something instinctual told her to veer to the left. She continued running for the next five minutes and her instincts paid off. When she hit the dirt road she stayed close to the trees, but walked long it for about half a mile until she came upon a road sign. Someone was looking out for her.

The rickety, wooden post was tilted, like a car may have run into it and no one bothered to right it. When she read the various markers that pointed to towns this way and that, some of the town names were Dunmanaig, Glenmore, Coldarbreck and Balrannaig. The marker that pointed towards the town and castle she'd just run from was called Dalkirk. From the sound of the names, she was in Scotland.

With that realization, she was yanked from the vision and found herself back in the dimly lit training room. Killian was in Scotland. She didn't get up from the floor. She remained there, thinking about it all. If she told everyone tomorrow that she knew where Killian's castle was, they would want to go charging over there to end him and Morgana.

None of them knew their fate yet, but her. If she told them what she'd seen, told them of their death to try and keep them from going, they would only tell her that it was only a vision, there was a chance that it might not come true OR they would choose to go anyway and bring up their duty to protect her no matter the costs.

Her face scrunched up in distaste at the thought of any of them being willing to die for her. She didn't want that. The only logical thing to do at this point was to go there without them. With her being the only one that knew the location, they couldn't follow her. Either she was going to kill Killian and Morgana and end this on her own... or die trying, but at least she's the only one that would lose her life.

Before she went back to the apartment she snuck to the room where her and Zoriana hid the books and other objects they brought back from their studies with Brielle. As she stood in the dark room that was lit only by the moonlight that poured in, she realized Brielle would solve her other problem. The problem of how she would get to Dalkirk. Brielle could teleport her there. She finished ripping out the passages of the spells that would kill vampires and warlocks from the book, before she returned it to its hiding place. Sneaking a quick look out the door to make sure the coast was clear, she folded the pages and stuffed them down her pants. She would have put them in her bra, but she currently wasn't wearing one.

Back in the apartment she exchanged the sweats for jeans, her boots and her leather jacket and put the ripped out pages in a hidden inner pocket of the jacket. After she dressed, she stood over the bed watching Eli sleep. He was on his stomach so she couldn't see his face that well. It was probably for the best. At least if this was the last time they had together, it was memorable. She wished she could kiss him one more time, but she ran the risk of waking him. She tiptoed out of the bedroom.

In the living room, she sat at the counter and wrote a quick note. She swallowed the lump in her throat and wiped away the tears that were beginning to stain the note. Hopefully, in time he would forgive her. If she came out of this alive, she hoped he still wanted a life with her. In her mother's vision they were married. She wanted him to understand that's why she was doing this. She wanted that vision to become a reality.

Her fingers trembled as she folded the note and wrote his name on it. She pressed the paper to her lips and kissed it. Tears sliding down her face the entire time. When she got to the door, she turned and looked back once more.

***

Once she was outside Walker House, she breathed a huge sigh of relief. Every step she was afraid someone would catch her and ask her what she was doing. Since she couldn't teleport she walked part of the way until she could catch the bus to Brielle's. She wasn't concerned with the time. Brielle was going to help her.

An hour after she'd left Walker House, she was standing on Brielle's doorstep. She rang the bell and waited. For some reason she hadn't expected the warlock to be asleep, given it was the witching hour.

She rung the bell again and seconds later Brielle angrily threw the door open. "What?" She was full of attitude until her eyes landed on Willow.

Brielle wore a pink, silk robe, unbelted, over some shorts and a crop top. She stepped out on the porch and glanced around the street. "You came alone?" She looked back at Willow.

"Yes. I need your help."

Brielle pulled her into the house. "Don't stand out on the porch where people can see you."

"What are you talking about? Do you know what time it is?"

She shut the door and walked into the living room. Normally, they worked in the basement so this was the first time she'd been in Brielle's actual home.

"I need your help."

"I heard you the first time. It's not enough I'm helping you learn black magic? Now what do you want." Nervously, she flitted about the room.

Before Willow could tell her why she was there Brielle interrupted her. "I'm going to make myself some coffee. Want some?" The last part was said from the other room since Brielle was already on the move.

"Sure." She called out.

While she waited she began to pace the room. Brielle seemed like a bit of a pack rat. Books were everywhere: bookcases, the coffee table and the floor. She picked up one and read the title. The cover was dusty. She put it back down and wiped her hands on her jeans as she continued to move about the room. That's when something caught her eye. She looked back towards the direction of the kitchen where she could hear Brielle banging around.

When she realized that she wasn't in danger of being caught for snooping she went over to the shelf that contained a collection of photographs and picked up the one that caught her eye. The frame and picture were covered in a fine layer of dust. Using her fingers, she tried to wipe it away so she could get a better look. She squinted at the old picture. *Is that?*

"Nosy bitch."

Before she could turn around it was lights out.

***

Her eyes fluttered open and that's when she felt the pain. Oh boy, was she going to have a massive headache. She could feel a limp forming on the back of her head and tried to reach around and feel it, but her hand-eye coordination was crappy due to the blunt force trauma she'd endured.

That's right. Brielle had struck her in the back of the head with something. But why? She tried to move again. That's when she realized she was tied up.

Her memory was still a bit foggy. What had she been doing before she was knocked unconscious? She wiggled around trying to get herself free of the handcuffs or whatever bound her wrists.

"You've done well."

The minute she heard the voice, a chill ran up her spine. Morgana. The memory slammed into her with crystal clarity. That's who she'd seen in the photo before Brielle knocked her out, a teenage Morgana.

"You promised you would help me get my hereditary power back. Well here she is, but you haven't upheld your end of the deal." Brielle whined and stomped her foot like she was a toddler.

Willow struggled to free herself before they were back in the room, but when she turned her head to look in that direction, she was greeted with Morgana's smiling face. "Look who's awake?" She walked over and stared down at her, all the while that maniacal smile was plastered on her face. "Go night, night." Morgana cajoled like she was talking to a child. Willow tried to say something and Morgana silenced her with one word. "Addormio."

CHAPTER 16

Eli

ELI WOKE UP and stretched. He hadn't slept that well in a while. When he looked over to her side of the bed he guessed that despite him telling everyone they didn't have to train today, she'd headed to the training room anyway… or maybe he was going to get lucky and she was in the kitchen making him some of those delicious chocolate pancakes he liked.

"Willow?" He called out to her while he pulled a shirt over his head and walked into the living room.

No Willow.

He decided he'd head to the training room and drag her back to bed. If he played his cards right, maybe he could keep her in bed at least until the afternoon.

When he flung the door open expecting to find Willow, he found nothing but an empty room. A weird feeling started to settle in his gut. "WILLOW?" He tried to communicate with her telepathically. *Please answer me.*

Over the next two hours, he searched the kitchens, the library, the other room she'd used with Cosmo, the bedroom she used the first time she came to Walker House, the dining hall (even though she'd never been known to go there) and finally he searched the square. When she didn't turn up after his search he went to Phaedra's apartment.

"Why are you knocking on my door like you're the police?" The look on her face was lethal until she saw the look on his face. "What's wrong?" She pulled him inside and finished pulling the belt of her robe tightly around her waist.

"Did you get rid of him?" Max walked into the room in his boxer briefs.

"Willow's missing." He told the two of them, trying not to sound bereft. Maybe Willow was safe and sound, but it wasn't like her not to answer him. Sure she'd been secretive lately, but to just up and disappear.

"Are you sure you searched everywhere?"

He nodded. His mind was reeling with the fact that she might be gone, but where. How could Killian or Morgana have gotten to her here in the house?

"Let us get dressed and then we'll take you back to the apartment. We can decide what to do next or if we need to widen our search. Plus, we can let the other Protectors know what's going on. Maybe they'll be able to help."

While he waited on the sofa for Phaedra and Max, he couldn't help thinking about how wonderful last night had been. They hadn't been this close in a month and now to wake up and she's gone, it was surreal. Maybe he'd wake up and find this was all just a nightmare and she was lying beside him sleeping.

When they got back to his apartment, Max went to the refrigerator. "Do you want me to make coffee? We might all think a little clearer with some caffeine to wake us up." He knew Max meant well, but he couldn't think about anything. He was consumed with finding out what happened to Willow. Phaedra rubbed his back and nodded at Max to make the coffee.

"Um... have you seen this?"

Eli looked up and found a folded piece of paper dangling from Max's fingers. He shook his head.

"It has your name on it."

He got up and went into the kitchen with Phaedra on his heels. Max handed him the note. Instantly, he recognized Willow's handwriting. Phaedra and Max were crowded around him, peering over his shoulder as he opened the note.

Dear Eli,

Last night was beautiful. I want more of that with you, which is why I have to go take care of this on my own. Please try and understand, I did this for us so that hopefully, we can have a future together. I didn't want anyone else to get hurt because of me. If I make it out of this alive, I hope you'll still want the future together that my mom saw for us.

I love you.

Willow.

He reread the note several times. When he finally stopped reading he walked into the living room and began pacing the floor, his mind was racing with questions. She left to go deal with Killian on her own? Was she out of her mind?

Phaedra and Max stood silently by, waiting for him to speak. They'd read the letter too, were they thinking the same thing he was?

"Someone helped her. We need to find out who helped her? How does she even know where to go?" He paused. Willow had a vision about Killian's location and kept it to herself. "Why wouldn't she tell us she knew where to find him?"

"Okay, stop for just a minute okay. You're rambling. We're not following along, because half of whatever you're thinking is in your head." Phaedra took a deep breath. "Who do you think helped her? Let's start there."

Someone knocked on the door before Eli could answer. Max went to answer it.

"I came as soon as I got the message." Zoriana stepped inside.

"Eli was just about to tell us who he thinks helped Willow get to Killian."

"What?"

Everyone turned to Zoriana.

"Didn't the message tell you that Willow was missing?" Phaedra was perplexed.

"No." Zoriana glared at Max. "It just said it was important that I get over here." She turned back to Phaedra. "How do you know that Willow went to find Killian?"

Eli handed her the note. "We don't think. We know. I think she had a vision recently that revealed his whereabouts and she left." He turned back to Phaedra. "There has to be something I'm missing. Why would she leave without us there to back her up?

"Maybe because she didn't want anyone else getting hurt." Zoriana's tone was full of anger. "In her note, she states that." She handed the note back to him.

"Someone helped her. We're all here so she couldn't have teleported. Maybe she was able to get a plane ticket or something. We need to get there and figure out if she bought a ticket headed anywhere."

"Why don't I teleport over there and see what I find?" Zoriana offered.

"Great." He was already heading towards the door. "We're going to pay the Elders a visit. This reeks of them."

***

It was clear that his father didn't appreciate being summoned. His robe billowed out behind him as he walked into the room. "What's the meaning of you calling us here for a meeting?" He bit out the words as he took his seat on the dais. The other Elders were assembling as well, some of them still trying to shrug into their robes.

"Willow is missing and I'm trying to find out if any of you helped her?" He didn't bother keeping the disdain from his voice as he took the time to glare at each of them.

"When you say missing, just what exactly do you mean? Do you think someone took her?"

He wasn't sure if his father was playing dumb to cover his own tracks or if the Elders truly had nothing to do with this. "She wasn't taken... she left to go fight Killian."

His father was up on his feet like someone had lit a fire under him. "Without the Protectors? She left to fight Killian without any of you? What if he turns her? The Congress will have our heads for this." Stepping down from the dais, he continued to rant. "Come with me. We must see Cora immediately."

There was a part of him that was unsure, but what else could he do. He was running out of theories and suspects. They followed his father to Cora's bedchamber. When they knocked on the door, the old woman's voice rang out clear as a bell. "Enter."

They filed into the room one by one. His father clasped his hands in front of him as he informed Cora of what had happened. Never one to register shock over a situation, she handled this like someone had given her a casual piece of news, such as, 'It's raining outside.'

When she was ready to answer she addressed him and not his father. "Eli, we must find out where she has gone at once. Nothing can happen to her or it could mean the end of everything that we know."

He knew Cora was right, but now that he knew the Elders had nothing to do with her disappearing act, it was out of answers.

A thought struck him and his face lit up with joy. "I think I may know how to find her."

"How? Tell us."

Ignoring his father's impatience, he addressed everyone. "I gave Willow a dagger. Before I gave it to her I put a tracking spell on it."

Cora smiled. Everyone seemed relieved. Eli let out the breath he'd been holding ever since he realized she was missing. "Indagare pugione."

After he said the words, a brightly colored arrow began to track along the floor. He began to follow it and everyone save Cora followed him out the door and through the square. Where was it going to lead them? Maybe he should stop and grab his jacket or wallet? No. If he needed those things he would conjure them later. When he thought the arrow was about to lead them outside, it turned the corner towards the apartments. Maybe she'd gotten cold feet and was hiding out somewhere.

Before he knew it they were back at his door. Did her common sense return and she came home. He pushed the door open and went inside. She wasn't in the living room. The arrow pointed towards the bedroom. Everyone followed him into the bedroom. The arrow pointed to the closet. When he opened the door, there lay her dagger on top of a pile of clothing. The one way he could have tracked her was lying on the floor of the closet.

Everyone backed up and gave him room when he turned around and stalked into the living room. He felt powerless, helpless, frustrated and angry. Willow could be at the mercy of Killian right now and there was nothing he could do about it. He flipped over the coffee table and yelled.

At that moment the door opened. Everyone swung their head around to see who would enter. Zoriana stepped inside and looked at the mess on the floor. Eli looked at her expectantly. His face fell the minute she shook her head. "There's no trace of her."

He dropped onto the sofa and held his head in his hands. What more could they do?

"I think I know who might have helped her."

Slowly, he lifted his head from his hands and gave Zoriana a dangerous look.

CHAPTER 17

Willow

WHEN SHE WOKE up this time, she was stretched out on an enormous, four-poster bed. She didn't need a sign or anyone to tell her where she was; she'd seen enough of Killian's horrible taste in décor from her dreams and visions to know she was in his castle. Thankfully, she wasn't gagged, but she was still shackled and this time her ankles were also bound.

She glanced around the room. Besides the oversized armoire, armchair and end table, there wasn't much in the way of furniture. Her second perusal of the room still showed no escape routes. She did her best to feel around and search her pocket to ensure the torn out pages were still on her pocket. Thankfully, the talisman Eli had gifted her was still on her wrist. She was so glad she hadn't forgotten it in her haste to leave Walker house.

Well now was her chance to try out the magic that she'd been learning. She aimed her finger at the shackles around her ankles. "Recludo." She rotated her ankles and wiggled her feet to get the circulation flowing.

"Well it looks like you saved me some time."

Her eyes darted over to the doorway, where Katana stood. *Fucking vampires. Can never hear when they're coming.*

Katana came over and hoisted her up from the bed like she weighed nothing. "Someone's waiting to see you." The smile she bestowed on her looked like the smile of some deranged serial killer, which technically, Katana was.

Willow allowed herself to be dragged to the throne room. She knew that's where Killian would be waiting to receive his prize.

When they entered a black hooded figure stood beside him. Katana marched her up the red aisle runner. Willow almost laughed at how cliché it was. As they came to a stop, the person removed the hood. Morgana gave her a smile reminiscent of her days as a Protector, before she became a traitorous murderer. So that's who'd been hiding under that hood in her vision. Did Morgana know she needed to hide so that she wouldn't see her in a vision?

After she glared at Morgana, she finally turned her attention to the bane of her existence... the Vampire King himself, Killian. He was dressed just as sharply as he always was when she saw him in a vision. She offered him no smiles, not even scowl. She just simply stared at him blankly.

"Willow, I've waited so long." His eyes perused her body. "I hope you found your room to your liking since I think you'll be staying a while." He stepped down off his throne and approached her. She was transported back to the day everything changed, when she'd woken up that morning from the terrible nightmare where he said her name for the first time. How terrified she'd been. The small ball of fear presently curled up in her belly like a snuggly kitten; paled in comparison to the terror she felt that day.

He raised his hand and caressed her face. His touch was cold. She wanted to flinch, but she wouldn't give him the satisfaction. "So, how's it coming with the Book of Prophecy?" She kept her tone casual.

Anger briefly flashed across his face and then it was gone in an instant. "Well now that you're here that won't pose a problem anymore." He raised his eyes to meet Katana. "Our guest needs something nicer to wear for dinner. See that the dress I picked out is brought to her rooms."

Willow hoped the trepidation she felt didn't show. She knew the dress he spoke of because she'd seen it. He moved closer and whispered in her ear. "Darling, you're trembling. I hope it's not because of me."

The man was toying with her. She still wouldn't give him the satisfaction. Her lips remained firmly closed.

"Take her to her room. I'll be there shortly." He seemed irritated that she wasn't responding to all of his little jabs. Inwardly, she smiled, while Katana took her back to her room.

After she left her, a few minutes later another vampire delivered a large gift box with ribbon tied around it. Without a word they dropped it off and left.

She knew the dress was waiting for her in that box, but she was in no hurry to put it on. Then she remembered he would be here to get her for dinner. There was no way she wanted to endure having to dress in front of him if he came down here and she wasn't dressed. Thankfully, Katana had unshackled her before she left. She went in the bathroom and showered. When she came out and finally untied the ribbon and lifted the lid of the box, the red silk from her vision stared up at her. She swallowed and tried not to think about it. Along with the dress, she found undergarments as well. He'd thought of everything. *How thoughtful.*

Right as she was trying to figure out how she would get the back zipper up, Killian entered the room. "Let me help you with that."

She didn't bother trying to tell him no, because she knew he would do as he pleased. His icy fingers made her skin crawl. He made it a point to run his finger along her skin as he zipped her up. Their eyes locked and held in the mirror. "You're beautiful."

At his words, her flesh crawled. So far it was all happening exactly like it had in the vision. When she looked at their reflection in the mirror, Killian wearing his tailor-made tuxedo and her in the floor length, strapless, red silk dress that hugged her curves just right, she thought they looked like a high-end ad for some chic perfume.

He was standing so close behind her. When he breathed on the back of her neck, it pebbled with gooseflesh. His hand settled on her hip and it took every ounce of willpower she had not to jerk away from his intimate touch.

"I'm hungry." He said as he ran his nose up the column of her throat. The sexual arousal mingled with the ravenous hunger she could hear in his voice.

A scream was building up in her throat. Was it all going to end here? Is this where he turned her?

"We should go eat." He pulled away from her and adjusted his cufflinks. When he turned his back, she let out a whoosh of air. Tears stung her eyes and she fought to keep them from falling. She wanted to cry out of sheer relief that her neck was still intact. "Come darling." He held out his arm to her like they were a couple going out on the town for an evening and not captor and captive.

She hated feeling like a puppet on a string, as she obeyed his command and took his offered arm.

In the dining room was a long table. Dinner had been set up at one end of the table where there were three chairs. He escorted her to her seat and like a gentleman pushed her chair in for her once she was seated. It was all so civilized. She hated this charade. Why didn't he just show his truth self and get this over with?

Killian took his seat and lifted the silver dish cover that kept her food warm. It was a bloody steak that looked like it was still mooing, fingerling potatoes and asparagus. Had she been served Killian's meal? When he uncovered his own dish, she blanched. If it was possible, his steak was bloodier than hers. She swallowed down the bile that rose up her throat.

He dug into his food with gusto. She couldn't stand to watch him eat. All she could think about was the vision where he feasted on her neck. She moved the knife and fork around to give the appearance that she was doing something. If the vegetables hadn't been sitting in the blood from the steak, she would have eaten them.

About ten minutes later, Morgana came in and sat in the third seat. She'd been wondering whether it would be Katana or Morgana that joined them. Part of her wanted to sip the wine that was being served, but she needed to remain sharp. She picked up the water glass and took a small sip.

"As you know Willow, the Book of Prophecy has been in our possession..." He took a sip of his wine. "We've been unable to open it and thought you might be able to shed some insight into how to open it." He glanced at her.

That was very presumptuous of him. Did he really think she'd just tell him how to open the book because she was his prisoner? She could have almost laughed out loud. The brazenness she felt wouldn't let her keep quiet. "And somehow you thought you'd dress me up, serve me dinner," she tossed her fork onto the plate, "and I would just tell you how to open the book?" When she said it out loud it actually did sound comical. She cackled. "If that was your idea of a joke. Please tell me more." She continued to giggle as she picked up her wine glass again and took a sip.

Morgana looked like she was ready to dive across the table and choke her out. Something passed between them and Morgana resumed her composure, eating her food in little bites. Killian kept eating his food as well... and then seconds later she found her head yanked back in an uncomfortable angle. He was pulling so tightly, tears were gathering in the corners of her eyes.

"Willow, I can be a reasonable man, but you're making me want to be very unreasonable. I asked very nicely for you to tell us what we wanted to know." He stroked and petted her face and hair. "I'd hate to have to get nasty about things."

The wicked smile she'd seen so many times in her dreams crossed his face. The thing was she wasn't the same person she was then. She knew he needed her. If he killed her he'd never gain access to the Book of Prophecy. "I'll never tell you." She spit the words at him defiantly.

Immediately, Killian seized her head between his hands and sent waves of pain spiraling through her. She screamed in agony. It went on for endless minutes before she finally passed out.

CHAPTER 18

Eli

MAYBE THE OTHERS could excuse Zoriana's poor judgment and blame it on her grief, but he wasn't sure he could. So far the Elders hadn't decided if they would punish Zoriana or not. Her fate was left up in the air until everything with Killian and getting Willow back was resolved.

Zoriana was there in the training room when he'd said no to learning black magic. Of all the people, he'd expected her to uphold that. To learn that she'd gone along with willow's zealous plot to fortify themselves with black magic so they could kill Killian and Morgana had infuriated him. Had that been Willow's plan all along? Learn black magic, abandon the team, abandon them and go after Killian on her own?

Unfortunately, he didn't have time to dwell on it or keep thinking about it. Only once they found her would he be able to ask questions. Currently, they were waiting on Brielle to open the door. Zoriana hung out on the lawn with Delaney and Evie, giving him a wide berth.

Impatient to know Willow's whereabouts, Eli knocked on the door again. Brielle was taking her sweet precious time answering the door.

"What do you want?" She flung the door open and stopped in her tracks when she saw the rest of the Protectors standing on the lawn.

Eli pushed her back into the house and everyone followed him inside.

"This is my house. You think you can just come in here..." Brielle yelled.

"That's exactly what I think." He motioned for Zoriana to come closer. When Brielle saw her, her eyes went wide in surprise. "You've been teaching her and another woman black magic. We believe that woman came to see you last night and you're going to tell us where you took her." He folded his arms across his chest and glared at her.

"I don't know what you're talking about. No woman came here."

His father stepped forward and when she saw his face she looked nervous.

"Brielle Campbell, formerly Brielle Walker before you were stripped of your hereditary magic for your participation in the Black Magic Rebellion. You will tell us what we want to know or I will have you brought before the Congress of supernatural Beings and trust me they will take more than your magic if something happens to the Oracle.

She swallowed as she stared at him coldly. "Fine, If I knew where she was I would tell you, that bitch, Morgana stiffed me after all I've done for her. I was going to tell her that the girl had learned some powerful spells that could be used against her, but when she screwed me over I figured she'd figure it out soon enough."

"Morgana took her?" Eli forcefully grabbed her arm.

She yanked her arm out of his grasp. "Yeah."

Phaedra stepped forward this time. "Where did she take her? If we have to ask again, it won't be so pleasant." Max stepped behind Phaedra and growled at Brielle. The defiant look on her face was slowly being replaced with a fearful look as Max continued to growl low in his throat.

"Okay. Okay. Just call off your attack dog... I'll tell you." Brielle relented. "Morgana took her to Scotland. I only know the country, not the city... she didn't trust me with that information." Brielle delivered the last part with a bitter tone.

"I guess when you're an opportunist yourself it's easy to spot one." Max glowered at her.

Two of the Council guardsmen entered the house and seized Brielle. She began to resist them, pushing and shoving. "I told you what you wanted to know. I helped you." She hissed and spit and tried to free herself from the shackles they were placing on her, that would keep her from using magic against them.

Silas addressed her. "You also committed a crime by conspiring with Morgana. Not only that, we can't have you warning her that they are coming for her." He motioned to one of the guards. "Take her away."

As they all filed out of the house, Eli was in quiet reflection. Willow had come here looking for help and been ambushed. There was no doubt that if Morgana took her, then Killian had her. The clock was ticking and all they had was a country.

"Get out of your head." Phaedra pulled him from his thoughts.

Eli began to voice his concerns aloud. "It's just... it's certain that Killian has her now. He's had her for hours at this point and all we have is a country. We have no idea where in that country." He was resisting using the word 'hopeless'.

Before he could say anything further, Max spoke up. "Yes, it seems daunting, like finding a needle in a haystack, but we're going to find her." Max grinned.

He could definitely use some of Max's perpetual optimism right about now. He nodded and gave a weak smile of thanks.

"Well, you should get going, teleport there and report back when you can. If you find you need some help or back up, let the Elders know and we'll reach out to covens in either Edinburgh, Glasgow or Inverness for help." Silas was leaving, when something made him hesitate. He turned and faced Eli. "I want you to know that I have complete faith that you'll get her back."

Eli was dumbfounded by his father's praise, even more so when he put his hand on his shoulder and squeezed. It appeared that he smiled at him too, but it looked a bit more like a grimace. Immediately afterward, he turned and disappeared.

Not looking to call attention to what just happened, he looked around at his team. "Everyone ready to go? It looks like we're headed to Scotland. Let's make our landing point in Edinburgh at Arthur's Seat. That way we won't call attention to ourselves by teleporting onto a crowded street or something. From there, it should only be anywhere from thirty to sixty minutes to get into the city."

They all agreed and one by one they disappeared. Eli was the last to teleport.

**

The wind was a bit brusque, as he walked towards Phaedra on the extinct volcano. "It looks like everyone's accounted for."

They stood at the edge of Arthur's Seat, and looked out at the city of Edinburgh. Its lights shimmered below as dusk settled across the sky.

"I think we're going to need help. Not only from some of the local covens, but we should call in the people we know and trust as well..." It wasn't hard to believe that if Killian had Morgana doing his bidding that he might not have a local witch or coven helping him out. "Who knows what exactly we'll be up against or how heavily fortified Killian's castle will be. Plus, we'll have Morgana to contend with." After he relayed the information he turned to Phaedra. "Let's get started."

CHAPTER 19

Willow

A SLIGHT TREMOR ran through her body as she sat up. Her vision blurred from the headache, a remnant of Killian's torture. Night had fallen while she was unconscious. Her legs wobbled when she stood. She dragged herself over to the mirror to do inventory. *Still in one piece.* For how much longer, she wasn't sure. She didn't think her body could endure too much more of what Killian was dishing out. And what was to stop him from finally just turning her to get what he wanted.

She went to the bathroom and grabbed a towel to wipe her bloody nose. She needed to rid herself of the silk dress and formulate a plan. If she was going to kill Killian and Morgana, it was going to have to be tonight.

Thankfully, her clothes were right where she'd left them when she undressed earlier for dinner. She exchanged the dress for her jeans and tank top. After she was dressed, she pulled the ripped pages from the black magic book from her leather jacket, and sat on the bed. Flattening her palm over the parchment to smooth it out, she looked at the spells. How was she going to use these, let alone get close enough to use them?

Plan. Plan. I need a plan. She began mouthing the words to the spells, to memorize them. Her brain was working on overtime trying to come up with something that would work and hopefully not get her killed in the process. She didn't think vampires slept, but the place did seem awfully quiet.

As the thought of sleeping vampires played in her mind, a memory of something Cosmo said during training came to her. *It helps if you try to take possession either when they're unconscious or asleep.*

That's how she was going to get this to work. She needed to take possession of Morgana and use her body, since she was more powerful with black magic. If she was in Morgana's body chanting these spells, she could win. Of course it sounded so easy in her head. She only had to get inside Morgana's body and manage to possess her long enough to kill Killian and his minions and then manage to get back in her own body. *Piece of cake.* The other question that arose was what would she do with Morgana after she'd killed the vampires? Once she returned to her body,

Morgana would be Morgana once again, and she would be on the warpath.

At this point, she could only cross one bridge at a time. If this plan stood even the smallest chance of working, she needed to take possession of Morgana tonight, and carry out her plan.

For the next ten minutes she studied the spells and committed them to memory. After she was sure she knew them, she lay back on the bed and began to do all of the things that Cosmo instructed her to do to ready herself to leave her body. In her mind, he was there repeating the steps to her.

"Relax. Deep breath..." She exhaled slowly. *"Now close your eyes."* Cosmo's voice told her. *"Clear your mind."* Last time, she froze at that, but this time she did exactly that. *"Slow down your heart rate. Focus on the beats and count in your head until the rhythm starts to match."* Unlike the last time, it took her a bit longer to slow her heart rate.

Her nerves were getting the best of her. "Stop Willow. Get it together. Your life depends on it." She spoke aloud to herself and then resumed attempting to slow her heart rate. Finally, her heart rate began to slow

"Think about death and let your consciousness drift away." Cosmo's voice instructed.

Minutes ticked by and soon she felt her spirit, pulling, tugging to be free. She didn't fight it. Her soul climbed from her body. It turned and looked at her now unconscious, technically dead self. If she was going to get back to her body she needed to complete her mission. She went in search of Morgana.

Her spirit prowled the castle, walking along the dimly lit hallways. She needed to find Morgana's room and find it fast. It felt like she'd been searching forever. After getting lost and visiting one area more than once, she had grown frustrated.

Finally, she ended up in another wing she hadn't been in yet. At the end of the hall, she saw light glowing beneath one of the doors. She went towards it and passed through the door.

The good news was she'd found Morgana. The bad news was Morgana wasn't asleep. Her mission had just become ten times harder, but she couldn't give up now.

Morgana stood in front of a full-length mirror brushing her hair. It looked like she'd just finished taking a shower.

Willow took a deep breath and recalled Cosmo's words once again. *"When your spirit pushes into the host body it's going to feel weird and strange at first because it's foreign to you, but keep going until you're securely lodged. Possession isn't easy. They will resist and try and keep you from coming in. You'll have to fight your way in. Be forceful."*

With her target in her sights, Willow took a running start and charged into Morgana's body. *Please let this work.*

To Be Continued

***

Continue The Oracle Chronicles Series
in the final novel, Divined.
https://www.moniboyce.com/series/oraclechronicles

Keep up with Moni's releases by joining her newsletter!
www.moniboyce.com

Also By Moni Boyce:
Redemption of the Heart

ACKNOWLEDGMENTS

First and foremost, I want to thank God, because without him none of this would be possible. I'm grateful to have the time and means to do something I love and I love storytelling. I've enjoyed specifically telling Willow and Eli's stories and sharing their journeys. It's been so much fun.

I want to acknowledge and thank my family and friends for always supporting and encouraging me. My parents and my sisters are so supportive and encouraging. I appreciate their understanding when I tell them I must disappear into my writing cave for a while. It means a lot to have them in my corner. Special thanks to my sister, Desi, for catching all the instances where I forgot to use a comma. I'm terrible when it comes to commas.

Again, I just want to send a huge shout out to Mallory Rock who designed the covers for the series because she did a phenomenal job. They are beautiful.

A really big thank you and shout out to all of my readers. You guys rock for buying and reading this book, the series. I truly hope you haven't been disappointed. I hope you enjoy it enough to buy and read the final book in the series and check out my other books. I know there are lots of ways you could spend your money and your time and it means a lot that you chose to spend it reading my book. You have my gratitude.

Disclaimer: Scottish town names used towards the end of the book are made up.

What Did You Think of Empowered: The Oracle Chronicles?

*First of all, thank you for purchasing this book **Empowered: The Oracle Chronicles.** I know you could have picked any number of books to read, but you picked this book and for that I am extremely grateful.*

I hope that it added value and quality to your everyday life. If so, it would be really nice if you could share this book with your friends and family by posting to Facebook and Twitter.

If you enjoyed this book and found some benefit in reading this, I'd like to hear from you and hope that you could take some time to post a review. Your feedback and support will help me as an author to greatly improve my writing craft for future projects and make this book even better.

*I want you, the reader, to know that your review is very important and so, if you'd like to **leave a review**, all you have to do is go to Amazon, Goodreads or Bookbub or the site where you purchased the book. I wish you all the best in your future success!*

About the Author

Moni Boyce is a writer, filmmaker, poet and author of contemporary and paranormal romance. She spent the last fifteen years working in the film industry and now creates characters of her own and brings them to life on the page. Moni has ghostwritten romance novellas and novels for over a year now and decided to put some of her own creations out in the world. She considers herself a bookworm, film buff, foodie, music lover and an avid world traveler having visited 33 countries and counting. She lives a bit of a nomadic life, but considers Los Angeles home. Which is the subject of her first travel book: Greater Than A Tourist – Los Angeles, California: 50 Travel Tips From A Local. Learn more about her at www.moniboyce.com

http://www.facebook.com/MoniBoyceWrites
http://www.twitter.com/MoniBoyce
http://www.bookbub.com/authors/moni-boyce
http://www.goodreads.com/moniboyce
http://www.instagram.com/moniboyce